I0747232

Mistletoe on Main Street

Holly Schindler

Mistletoe on Main Street

Published by InToto Books

Copyright © 2025 by Holly Schindler

Cover design by Holly Schindler

Fonts: Alice and Cupid designed by Aurelie Maron; Highway Gothic designed by Ash Pikachu Font (DaFont)

Ruby's Place Stories

**EXPERIENCE THE MAGIC OF THE
ORIGINAL
RUBY'S PLACE COLLECTION**

Christmas at Ruby's
I Remember You
Sentimental Journey
The Gift That Is Ruby's Place

**RETURN TO THE MAGIC IN
THE SPINIOFF SERIES
RUBY'S REGULARS**

Ruby's Story
Rare Gems
Tinsel Town
A Troublesome Heart
Mistletoe on Main Street

ONE
Last Year

T‍HE DOOR TO MATTHEWS'S OFFICE flew open, hitting the wall with the sharp crack of a snare drum.

A-rum-pa-pum-pum, Russ caught himself thinking sarcastically, even as the vibrations from the impact still rippled through his chair and up his spine.

His coffee cup hovered next to his bottom lip, steam warming the tip of his nose. One of his favorite things about this particular newsroom was the coffee. Brewed with a real percolator, not one of those electric things that only made swill that reminded him of sweat socks at the gym. Real percolator coffee, a deep, thick, dark brown, so strong it was just nearly bitter but never actually was. That was his favorite flavor of anything, that razor line before bitter.

Hard to believe the rest of the newsroom liked their coffee the same way. And yet, for the past six years, that was all their break room had ever had. A fresh pot waiting right there for the taking.

"Keegan!" Matthews bellowed, Russ's last name now vibrating through his bones. Matthews was a bit of a sitcom version of an editor, with his balding head and his perpetually loosened, crooked necktie, his sloppily rolled shirtsleeves, his hands on his hips, the large curve of his belly.

And the scowl. Which he was never seen without. And that last name thing. It was always just Matthews. Somehow, he didn't seem like a person who should have ever had a first name. Never, not once in the six years that Russ had worked at this particular paper, had there ever been a time when Matthews had spoken of his home life (Russ had no idea if he was even married or not), or hummed a favorite song under his breath. He had not smoked, or popped his knuckles, or revealed any other sort of humanizing bad habit. He had also never given a single reporter any leeway regarding a deadline (Russ's personal preference—he liked the rush of meeting a concrete deadline with less than three minutes to spare). Russ had never so much as seen the tiniest hint of a smile from Matthews. There was just nothing personal about him.

Jim from sports winced in sympathy. Jim was a byline vet like Russ, the sort with gray flecked through his beard. They had gravitated toward one another from Russ's first day on the job. It had been good to have a friend in the newsroom. It didn't always happen that way. In fact, Russ had once tried to remember how he and Jim had introduced themselves to one another, but no such memory had ever surfaced. It was more like the two of them had always been friendly. Like all the years before knowing each other were more like a pause before seeing each other again. Funny how some people just fit like that. Like...

Well. Come to think of it, that had never actually happened to Russ before.

Russ put his cup down without taking a sip. No need to ruin a good cup of coffee with whatever Matthews was about to unleash on him.

As he stood, his eyes only barely glanced at his keyboard, a sea of gray squares. He'd long ago rubbed the letters off from all the typing, and the only ones with any of the white labels left were the rarely used escape and function keys.

"Before I start collecting my social security, Keegan," Matthews growled, mostly, Russ knew, as a way to put on a show for the rest of the reporters. Tight ship and no questioning his demands and all the rest of that sitcom-style barking that was so like Matthews.

Russ grabbed his sweater off the back of his chair. Matthews's office was always a meat locker. As he shrugged into it, he caught sight of the snow outside his window. Funny how it was pitch black and yet the snow nearly glowed it was so bright white. Must have somehow been reflecting the light from inside the newsroom, Russ caught himself thinking as he tugged his shirt sleeves down beneath his sweater, taking a few beats to watch it fall.

Yes, in Russ's mind, the snow fell. It didn't dance or trickle or swirl. No need for fussy, frilly words when something straightforward would do.

Patricia, the newest hire, blushed as he passed. Averted her eyes, too. Almost like some damsel out of a silent movie. The shy girl who can't come right out and admit her crush but also doesn't want to pretend it doesn't exist or potentially discourage said object of the crush from making his move.

Poor Patricia. She didn't know that Russ was done with all that. With crushes and love and dating. But it was nice to still be thought of that way, especially by a woman who had to be nearly twenty years his junior.

Josie used to tease him about liking attention from other women too much. Didn't everyone, secretly, deep down? No matter how in love you already were with someone else?

He veered off closer to an external wall, away from Patricia's desk, and found that the constant tapping in his ears, a steady at the newsroom, only intensified. *Was* the incessant soft clicking the sound of fingertips throughout the newsroom, each pair of hands racing to meet deadlines? Or had the precipitation outside begun to turn to sleet?

Russ wasn't exactly in the mood for sledding home. Sledding, hot cocoa, tinsel…the plastic parts of Christmas made his feet itch like he needed to start running. Six years ago, maybe there had been a chance that he would not have become yet another middle-aged humbug. Maybe there had still been a flicker inside of him, some instinct to see Christmas differently. Six years ago, maybe something warm and tingly had even stirred in the deepest part of him. Something that could have been the Christmas spirit. But this year, a full six years after losing his Josie on Christmas Eve, he was content to put on his blinders so he didn't have to see the obnoxious sale signs and automated, dancing Santas and those awful shiny, pre-made bows you were supposed to buy in bulk and stick on presents.

Yes, plastic. That was the word he leaned on. But the truth was, Russ knew there was joy out there. Not all Christmas was fake. The joy part was real. It was just that joy was gone now, for Russ. So all that was left were a bunch of faded Santas with white plastic beards that reminded Russ of shredded Walmart bags.

At least, Russ thought as he snaked his way between his colleagues' desks, each of them chipped and scuffed and beaten from the grind of pounding out daily headlines, he would not be forced to endure a holiday party. A man like Matthews did not go for that sort of thing. Not ever. And here, the day before Christmas Eve, no one else in the office was going to go suggesting some awkward Secret Santa exchange or plunk a tin of home-made cookies on the edge of his desk and grin in that sickening way that said, *Now your turn.*

Yes, the danger had passed. Yet again. Year six. No lit-up ties. No radio tuned to one of those all-day caroling marathons. And no schmaltzy human-interest assignments. As Russ closed in on Matthews' office, Jim made it a point to pass him on his way to the copier. Flashed a grimace. Russ only shot him a look back that said it would be fine, whatever it was. He could endure whatever chewing out Matthews had in mind. The man could tear his recent work to bloody shreds and roar that he should be demoted to writing pet obituaries for the Pennysaver. It was all endurable as long as Russ did not have to crank out some sort of holiday memories clap-trap.

Matthews was drumming his fingers on the desk like he'd been waiting for Russ for the better part of De-cember as he slipped through the open doorway.

"Need you to go to Sullivan," Matthews said, motioning for Russ to shut the door.

Russ's stomach behaved as though he had just sped downhill on a sled. One of those plastic disks with no brakes. "Sullivan?"

"Yeah," Matthews growled. "Somebody's gotta investigate this tip."

Relief warmed Russ, even in the chill of Matthews's office. A tip. That didn't sound like fluff. "Mayoral corruption?" He attempted to beam, but it was hard when his voice sounded pitiful and far away, like some poor whimper at the bottom of an empty well, a plea for help.

"No corruption. Nothing political at all." Matthews flopped back in his chair. The screws screeched against his weight. "I hate to burden you with this garbage, but you're the one with no family. Won't mind a Christmas Eve assignment, will you?"

Russ cleared his throat and sat up straighter in the chair on the other side of Matthews's desk, the one that had always looked to him like it had been squirmed in by a nervous cub reporter with a box cutter in his back pocket. "Christmas Eve?" Russ parroted, his voice buried beneath the clatter of Matthews suddenly digging through his bottom desk drawer.

"Wouldn't give it so much as a second thought, usually," Matthews admitted, "but circulation's down. We could really use a boost. Some of that human-interest drivel. Hate sending my best reporter to cover it. Kind of like sending Cronkite to cover a kitten's oak tree rescue." He wasn't even looking at Russ. Did he not have the guts?

"What—?" Russ tried. "What's the actual—?" Everything inside of him ached. He felt like a human-sized canker sore.

"Supper club. In Sullivan, Missouri. What's the name…" Matthews tugged his attention from the drawer long enough to riffle through some of the papers scattered on his desk.

"Ruby's Place," Russ tried. But his voice completely gave out on him.

"I just wrote it down," Matthews grumbled.

Russ felt it smash into him, painfully: the last time he had ever been happy. Six years ago, that Christmas Eve with Josie, in Sullivan. It hit him like some sort of horrific sucker punch, the kind of thing that happened in contrived melodramatic movies. Was this a joke? He had already run from Sullivan. Run from the loss and also from the knowing that came with that kind of loss. The knowing that recognized a lifetime never promised that kind of joy. Not even once. Happiness like he had known that Christmas Eve with Josie in Ruby's Place was neither recoverable nor repeatable. Once that kind of happiness shattered, it was gone.

The running had brought him here, to this city, this newsroom. Not far in miles, maybe, but how did you measure the distance of the heart? Whatever it was, this place was the equivalent of light years from Sullivan. All these years later, the ache wasn't gone, but at least he wasn't having to look at it face-to-face. And now—what?

Matthews was…he wasn't sending him back, was he? For what?

"Ruby's Place!" Matthews declared, finally finding his note-to-self. He returned to digging through that dumb drawer. Sounded like that thing had roughly twenty-three pounds of loose paperclips in it. Maybe a dozen or so random ball bearings for good measure.

"What—was the—tip?" Russ tried.

Six years ago, he and Josie had worked together, in another newsroom, one that had nothing to do with Matthews. And the last-minute holiday story that had brought them to Sullivan had been a retail worker walk-out. In the final shopping hours of Christmas Eve, no less. They had conducted their interviews and pounded out their story in the car, debating every last word choice as Josie typed it into her laptop. They'd tethered Russ's phone to gather up just enough of a signal to email it to the newsroom from the backseat a full twenty minutes to spare before their deadline. And then, at Josie's insistence, it was time to celebrate. Maybe not the story—it was not exactly Pulitzer Prize material—but certainly the holiday. And so they had driven, night having fully fallen, the holiday lights on all the businesses pouring through the windshield to outline Josie's profile in gold.

"*There*," Josie had insisted, pointing at the red Ruby's Place neon sign. He had been prepared to only humor her, but once he had stepped inside…oh, the *feel* of it. Russ had never been able to shake it off, no matter how far away he tried to tell himself his heart was. Just the two of them, dancing, because even in a crowded room there was no one else, just them, partners in stories and everything else, her laughter and the mistletoe she had stuck behind her ear, her long dark hair *cascading*. That was the exact word he had leaned on back then, the jasmine smell of her long hair in his nose. Back then, frilly words hadn't bothered him so much.

An out-of-nowhere Christmas Eve tornado warning had buzzed through their phones, interrupting their dance and creating a bit of a stir in the portion of the crowd closest to them. Always reporters, always powered by the instinct to be the first on the scene, they'd rushed to get back on the road, racing the wind. They had no way of knowing then they were in their last few minutes together, that they were about to become the story.

Or Josie would, anyway. In the most horrifically final way.

"Can you believe it?" Matthews wheezed, laughter spilling straight into the still-open drawer, mixing with all the loose keys he couldn't toss because he'd forgotten what they unlocked.

"Believe what?"

"Weren't you listening? That it's haunted."

"Ruby's Place?" Russ frowned. That night he and Josie had spent inside Ruby's had been filled with crystal chandeliers and linen tablecloths and piano music. And everyone there had been so dolled up. That was Josie's description, shouted into his ear. Heels and cufflinks, he remembered. And gifts being passed around, hand to hand. And singing that never stopped. One carol after another, barely enough of a pause between them for a breath. He had never quite forgotten the smell of the owner's homemade marshmallows, either, the ones Josie'd coaxed him into trying. He hadn't been able to stop, one after another, even though marshmallows had always been too sweet for him. Annoyingly sweet. What was the word he had used? Cloying, that was it.

Not that night, though.

"Are you sure you have that right?" Russ asked. "Haunted?" The place had been old, even six years ago, but in a vintage, mid-century way. Not in a Halloween cobweb sort of way.

"Well," Matthews admitted. "Not haunted exactly. I—there!" He finally unearthed an item from his drawer and held it up for Russ to see. The pride on his face was the first spec of emotion Russ had ever seen him wear.

"Is that a typewriter ribbon?" Russ asked.

"It is at that."

"I thought typewriter ribbon was too old-fashioned even for this place," Russ blurted. One of his favorite things about this current newsroom, and why he had so relentlessly pursued the job. He loved the seriousness of the atmosphere, the bare-bones, unfancy professionalism of it, the unrelenting buzz of everyone's pursuit of a better story. Better than anyone else's story, better than their own last story. It was hard to find a place like that. Every year, every job, a little harder than the last.

And here Russ had been, working at the same place for six years. He couldn't have dreamed up a luckier gig.

"Old-fashioned?" Matthews said. "I guess it is." His face went all calendar on Russ. That was how he'd always thought of it, anyway. That faraway expression people got when you were asking them to go back in their minds, back to some momentous thing that had happened to them. Usually, for the news, a somewhat traumatic event.

"If I had a nickel for every typewriter ribbon I changed out in my day," Matthews muttered. His face reflected the memories of stories circling through his head. For the first time, Russ saw the hint of something personal. He wasn't sure if he warmed to it or if it unnerved him.

"Anyway," Matthews said, "I thought maybe I could turn it into some sort of decoration."

"You what?"

"Yeah, sort of like tinsel or something. Maybe get one of those small tabletop trees and decorate it like a proper newsroom tree. Typewriter ribbon, press badges…"

"You want to *decorate*?"

"Why wouldn't I? It's almost Christmas."

"I just—I thought we were so close—and you—don't usually go—for that."

"Too bad you won't be here to see it," Matthews said.

Russ stared at him with an expression that could only be described as unmoored. Why wouldn't he be here? Matthews was really going to make him go?

"The locals out there, in—"

"Sullivan," Russ finished.

"Right. Sullivan. The locals apparently claim that on one night a year, Christmas Eve, the spirits come to life in Ruby's Place."

"The…*Christmas*…spirits?" Russ croaked. Talk about cloying.

"I know. Corny as all get-out," Matthews agreed. "They say—this tip, that is—it said that on Christmas Eve, you get a chance to finally see that one person again."

Russ's insides began to buzz in a painful way. Where had this story come from? He had been there. In Ruby's. It had been a holiday spectacle, but there had been no hint of this. Not some story about—what? "You can connect with the dead?" Russ asked. "That's what you're saying?"

"Not all dead. Just one dead. The one person who was important to *you*," Matthews said. "The one you thought was gone forever. You get to tell them whatever was left unsaid. You know—oh, I love you so much or I miss you or—"

"I'm so sorry." Russ whispered it, the one thing he would have said to Josie, given a chance.

But there would never be a chance. This tip of Matthews's was a total fabrication. A dumb schmaltzy piece of fiction, not unlike Santa Claus.

"What's that? What'd you say?" Matthew pressed, leaning over his desk, closer to Russ, as though to hear him better.

Russ shook his head in a *Nothing, never mind, not important* sort of way. But he felt a lot like that chair beneath him: torn to shreds by some invisible blade.

"Since this is all so last minute," Matthews said, "I did go ahead and make you a reservation. The Sullivan Inn. But since you'll probably pay through the teeth for anything else you'll need this close to the holiday, I wanted you to have this." Matthews held up the company credit card, the fluorescent office lights somehow dancing like white twinkle lights across the laminated front.

He slammed it on the desk in front of Russ, the whack echoing through the tiny office.

A-rum-pa-pum-pum, Russ thought.

Two

RUSS WAS NOT GOING to Sullivan.

He knew that, even as he apologized to his house-plant and logged into his postal service account to have his mail held.

No way was he going to Sullivan.

He paced in front of his wall-to-wall bookshelf of signed first editions, pausing to glare at the stack of new releases he had brought home for his holiday. Which was, for him, not really a holiday. Not anymore. A day off from work was all. His home had no Christmas tree to drop needles. Not a single Christmas card adorned his mantel. But the world would, in fact, shut down, and the books had been his grand plan for passing the time.

He had also picked up everything he needed for a special dinner: a roasted chicken thigh with rosemary and garlic, mashed potatoes with butter and cream, asparagus, a slice of cranberry chess pie from his favorite corner restaurant (the one that served the Southern dishes he had neither the time nor patience to make himself but always reminded him of eating at his favorite aunt's place), and a glass of Pinot Noir. An outsider looking in would have recognized it as the makings of a lovely Christmas Eve, especially for someone determined not to have a Christmas. He had even brought in a few logs for the fireplace, the one in the living room, because his ground-floor apartment was actually the former parlor of an old Victorian, the kind of place he had once told Josie he'd dreamed of owning. Big front porch, and a swing for reading.

Not Christmas, Russ would have insisted. *Just a few wintry moments of cozy, quiet comfort.*

And now? He would have to leave it all behind.

But just for a little while. Because he was not going to Sullivan.

He was only going as far as he would have to for a logical excuse. A detour. Some way to placate Matthews without having to tell the story. The real, horrible, painful reason why he was not going to Sullivan.

It was the last happy place he'd been with Josie.

16

That was it. That was the reason. A tale he had never told the impersonal Matthews or anyone else in the newsroom, for that matter. Russ had been so grateful—not for the secret, but for his ability to keep it. No one, not even Jim in sports, knew the tragic story that had brought him there. Now, though, Russ almost regretted his secret-keeping. If Matthews had known, he surely would not have sent him.

Russ was not going to Sullivan. He never would have returned to Sullivan, because he could not bear to come face to face with what had actually happened. Now, though? With this new story, this piece of fiction Matthews told him? This lie about Ruby's Place? It would only break his heart. The idea of it. Really. That you could meet up with the past? Settle it all? Russ knew himself well enough to predict that the story would light something inside of him. Something that would ache for the impossible. In that split second it took to cross the threshold, hope would find him. Hope that he really could see Josie again. And then, the reality of it not being true would destroy him all over again.

There was no settling this guilt. There was no place that a person could find that kind of peace.

Besides, even if the Christmas Eve legend of Ruby's Place was true, it didn't have to go well. What if the other person, the one you left behind, was in fact quite mad? What if the dead held grudges?

Would Josie be mad? Would she toss a drink in

his face? Scream, tell him everything she had missed out on, all because of him? All that time. She'd still had so much time.

Most importantly, why was he even thinking about it? Why would he even consider the possibility? He knew this story was nothing more than small-town gossip. A silly game of telephone that had finally reached his editor's desk. A complete fabrication.

And it didn't matter anyway, because he wasn't going to Sullivan.

He knew it, even as he tugged his overnight bag from the front hall closet. The small one just for toiletries. It let out a cough of protest as he jerked the zipper. The teeth were kind of warped and the zipper didn't slide well. He yanked back and forth, unsure why the bag had decided to unleash its own round of *will not*s. When he finally got it most of the way open, he tossed his razor and a can of shaving cream inside.

The can clinked.

Afraid the nozzle had somehow busted and cream was spewing all over the inside of his case, he grimaced and cautiously slipped a hand inside. The bag smelled musty and the leather felt dry. How long had it been since he'd last been on the road?

His fingers wrapped around a long, flat object. When he pulled it out, there it was—the mother-of-pearl clip Josie had always worn in her long chestnut hair.

That clip punched him in the gut. Made him put

a hand on his stomach, right above his belt. A handful of seconds ago, he would have been certain he didn't have any of Josie's own belongings. Not anymore. But here it was, the same clip he'd had a habit, once, of squeezing so it would release, to send her long hair tumbling about the sides of her face.

"*Give it back*," she would always insist, but in a singsong way that said she interpreted it as a playground tease. Saw the relic of the little boy in him, the one wreaking a tiny havoc on the girl he liked. Girls never understood why boys did that. But wasn't it only natural to pinch back once you had been pinched yourself? And didn't that first boyhood crush always feel like a pinch to the heart?

Only natural. Or so Russ had thought.

But by the time Russ and Josie were together, it wasn't a tease. It was Russ wanting to touch that glorious hair, the most stunning part of the most stunning woman he'd ever seen.

And he could do it. He could reach right up, take her hair down, and keep the barrette in his coat pocket. It made him feel good to know he was that guy. The one she smiled at as she put her palm on the part of her head now missing the clip as she moaned, "Hey," through a good-natured laugh.

He turned the clip over in his hand. Why was it so hard to throw it away? Had he encountered it before? Put it back where he'd found it? Surely he had. It couldn't have happened any other way. Too much time had passed. He would have bumped up against it anytime he needed his overnight case. And he *had* used it in six years. Of course he had. He hadn't spent the entirety of the past six years in that newsroom, clacking away at the keys. Even though the letters *were* all rubbed off.

But when? When was that last assignment that had sent him out on the road? It had not felt unusual for Matthews to be handing him a company credit card… had it? Certainly it hadn't felt like the first time.

But why were the details as foggy as cold mornings near the lake, the one where he and Josie had spent their weekends together? Playing house, that was how she'd put it. But to Russ, it had just been a way to create a world with only two people in it, no outsiders allowed.

He squeezed the hair clip so hard, the sharp edges of the metal clasp dug into his palm.

He could not stop staring at that bag. How could he not remember being on the road at any time in the last six years? But as he asked himself, he also immediately knew the answer. He had put his head down and gotten to work. Even on assignment in another location, he'd had blinders on. Glorious work. It was all he had seen the past few years. It had been a place to escape. To run from the grief.

A place to get away from Josie's memory.

And the wracking guilt. It was a way to get away from that, too. From knowing that he was the reason

Josie wasn't around anymore.

Even now, after the better part of a decade, his words were in his mouth, tumbling around like hot stones stuck to his tongue, too big to spit out: "We're less than twenty minutes from the heart of the storm," he'd insisted, that last Christmas Eve. "Come on. If we leave right now, we'll be there. In the impact zone. At the exact moment the clouds roll out." He'd had to yell it, so Josie could hear him over the din in Ruby's Place. "Christmas Eve tornado! It'll be picked up nationwide." His hand was on hers and he was leading her out the front door.

Had she pulled back against him? Sometimes, when that night came back to him, always against his will, it seemed she had. Had she moaned that it was late and she only wanted to spend the rest of their Christmas Eve right there, savoring their holiday treats, their hot cocoa, the carols, the voices, the crowd that did not feel like a collection of elbows but welcome, like a house packed tight with all your favorite people? Had she said something about having already covered the retail workers' strike? That they had done their job and they were entitled to a holiday?

That didn't seem right. Not really like Josie. But then again, maybe she'd had some sort of premonition. A vibration of warning somewhere deep inside, her own rolling thunder.

Shaking his head at himself, he dropped the clip into the pocket on his khakis. Turned his attention back to his closet.

Russ tossed a couple days' worth of clothes into his suitcase. And with one last look around at his empty apartment, he locked the door behind him.

But he was not going to Sullivan.

HE DID START his drive in the direction of the small town, of course. He had to, in order to enact the rest of his plan.

At a gas station ten miles or so from the Sullivan limits, he slammed a nozzle into his truck.

"Now," he said, tugging his phone from his pocket. "Time to find another story." He scrolled on his phone while the numbers flicked past on the gas pump. Surely, he thought, there was something. Just one syrupy-sweet story. Some Reddit thread. Some semi-viral post on Facebook. Something that could replace the Ruby's Place assignment.

He found a lost dog, a one-eyed pug named Carol, who had escaped from a backyard during the family's recent visit to their Aunt Joy's house, only to miraculously return home on little Scott's seventh birthday, one week to the date before Christmas. Little Scott was a horrible stutterer, but never with Carol, his very best friend.

It was a bit weak, honestly. Especially when compared to the supernatural splendor of meeting up with the dead. Settling things up with the loves of your life, ripped away too soon.

The better story was the one that Matthews had given Russ.

Or was it? Russ reminded himself it was a better story *if true*. But not if it was a lie. If a lie, Russ would have to go scraping up some sappy tidbit inside Ruby's, something equally weak. Maybe some widow had come to Ruby's Place looking to meet up with dearly departed husband number one and wound up meeting husband number two. Surely there were stories like that in there. But was that really any better than the gift of the return of a childhood dog? One who helped you communicate with the world?

He was certain he could make the dog thing work. It would have been slightly better if Scott had a Christmas name, too. But maybe, if he was lucky, the family would be willing to sit around the piano he saw in their living room Facebook photos. Wear their matching pjs and sing. And maybe Carol would toss her head back and howl. Scott's mother would say something like how it was a regular Christmas miracle. Just the kind of drivel they all avoided at the newsroom but Matthews now claimed they needed.

Russ messaged Scott's mother and she responded right away. "We'd love to be interviewed!" she said, following her message with several Christmas-themed emojis.

There, Russ thought. And he started his car. When he next talked to Matthews, he'd include a snowstorm, a dash of car trouble, maybe a road blocked by a fallen tree. Matthews would grunt in acceptance, understanding why Russ had to take the detour. And the next time Russ walked into the newsroom, Matthews would slap his shoulder and tell him only the consummate professional would be able to still get a story in on time, one crammed full with an appropriate amount of Christmas Eve schmaltz.

But before Russ shifted into drive, he pulled the hair clip from his pocket.

SNOW ASSAULTED Russ's windshield.

He rubbed at his face, his beard sharp against the palm of his hand. His phone pinged. Scott's mother wanting to know where he was, surely. She had asked three times already.

But he had gotten turned around. Must have been the flakes. Big fluffy things. Snow globe flakes.

Stupid things had probably been what had kept him from seeing his turnoff.

He drove and drove, wipers waving. They were

beginning to make him feel sick to his stomach, like the incessant swinging of an amusement park ride.

Russ hated amusement park rides.

He squinted, leaning still closer to the windshield. For a moment, he missed having a navigator. Josie barking at him which turn to take, all while singing to the radio. Some ancient blues tune. Somehow, Josie had known where all the blues stations were, no matter the state.

Ahead, a city limits sign.

Russ turned. But as his headlights washed across it, he realized it was made of rustic, knotted wood. And a cardinal had perched itself on the edge. Perfectly poised, like a Christmas card.

And the sign said, simply, "Sullivan."

Russ let out a frustrated growl. How could that have happened? How could he have gotten the kind of lost that had led him right back to the one place he was trying to avoid? How had he suddenly found himself in an episode of *The Twilight Zone*?

Still cursing at himself, he followed yet another sign, pointing toward the business district. Best way out of Sullivan, he figured, was through.

The flakes eased up, but his heart rate did not. It thudded and crashed inside his ears. His pulse throbbed against his skin.

Streetlights behaved differently as he entered Sullivan; they cast a stronger, warmer glow. They let Russ see everything along the streets: Plate glass windows painted up with smiling snowmen and dancing candy canes. White lights, all twinkling to the same rhythm. Tinsel wrapping every street sign. Vintage-looking aluminum snowflakes attached to light poles.

His grip let up on the steering wheel and his shoulders relaxed. He didn't want them to. He hadn't even expected them to. He chalked it up to the release associated with getting off the highway. He'd spent most of his driving life avoiding interstates and fast lanes.

He focused on the foot traffic, growing increasingly heavier the closer he grew to the square. And suddenly, he was part of it, easy as the slip into a favorite daydream: the shoppers, the packages, the voices. Music, faintly. Carols from car radios. Distant sleigh bells. Laughter. The town tree, glimmering like childhood memories.

Russ pulled to a stop in front of The Sullivan Inn. He had not remembered such a place when he and Josie had been here. There had, in fact, been nowhere to stay, not one hotel or B&B. And that was how they'd wound up at Ruby's Place. It had promised a moment of warmth. Somewhere to get a drink, rest a moment. Catch their breath, maybe even ask a few locals who might know a nearby town likely to have a bed for the night.

They hadn't expected to find the full-blown holiday spectacle that had greeted them behind the supper club's bright green door.

Russ sighed, staring up at the front of The Sullivan Inn. A small place, quaint, but more than a B&B. Someone had opened it up in the last few years, obviously. Place was beyond decked out, with white lights and red bows and garlands galore. Decorations pulsing like a vacancy sign, just begging somebody like Russ to help them turn a profit that holiday season.

All he wanted to do was keep driving. But it was the responsible thing to go inside and free up the room. The one Matthews had put a deposit on. Russ certainly wasn't going to use it. He had accidentally crossed the city limits, maybe, but he was not staying the night.

He kept his head down, away from the stars just waiting for wishes, and he slipped inside the front door of the inn.

"Well, hello!" the woman at the counter greeted. She was everything Hallmark insisted an innkeeper should be. Rosy-cheeked and middle-aged, with graying blond hair, ornament-shaped earrings, and a sweater vest littered with appliquéd holly sprigs.

"I..." Russ shook his head. "I think my editor called and made a reservation."

The woman nodded, held one of her index fingers into the air, and did a regular pirouette, spinning toward the wall behind her, where available keys hung on tiny little brass hooks.

"You don't have to do that," Russ tried. "I came in because I needed to cancel. I wanted to let you know.

Make sure that you weren't holding a room for someone who wouldn't use it."

"Here it is," the woman sang, pulling a key from the wall. She spun again, holding it in the air between herself and Russ.

But Russ's eyes were on the wall just behind the woman's shoulder. "How can you have so many keys still hanging there? This close to the holiday?"

"This is the hardest time to rent a room," she admitted. Her voice continued to echo after she spoke, a little like the ringing of a glass bell.

"Guess most people who come to Sullivan stay with family," Russ said. What was there about her that made him want to comfort her? Almost like a child that needed attention. He got the feeling he was dealing with some sort of pure heart that would be destroyed by any slight.

"Most people don't *see* us," she corrected.

"On the street here?" Russ asked. It was true that Sullivan was arranged like most small Midwest towns, the string of businesses all in turn-of-the-century red-brick, linked together down the street like paper dolls. Sometimes one storefront really could bleed into another.

"I found it just fine," he said. Still that desire to comfort her, for some reason.

"Well. You go on and head up now," she told him, her hand already on his shoulder as she led him toward the stairs. One of those elaborate staircases with the ornate, carved maple banisters and newel posts. "You're in Room 4. I thought you would like the view from there the best."

Russ was already scolding himself, even as his feet were moving toward the stairs. He had to get out of there.

"Oh, I haven't had anyone here since my Clarence…" She paused, then said, sheepishly, as though it were something unspeakable, "*went his way*." She wiggled her fingers, as though pantomiming a spirit breaking apart.

Was this why Russ had felt a need to comfort her all along? This thing they shared? Had he somehow felt it, even before she'd said it out loud?

She had to have just lost him. This Clarence person. If Russ was her first guest after his death. A death on Christmas. He knew what that was like.

Without a word, Russ climbed the stairs, lined with the kind of light colored floral wallpaper he had once seen in his grandparents' home.

He could stay one night. Contact Scott's mother, tell them he would be there early tomorrow morning. Christmas Eve day. Get it done and wrapped so he wouldn't interrupt their celebration. She'd told Russ already they wouldn't be traveling. Probably, for the boy and the dog, it would be far better to do it in the morning, especially since it was already getting late and Russ would now have to backtrack. They'd all be fresh tomorrow. Tonight, by the time he got there, the dog and the boy both would be worn out and grumpy.

He pulled out his phone to text Scott's mother. But stopped when he remembered what the woman at the desk had said. That he'd have the best view.

Curious, he walked to the window and tugged at the curtain—a flimsy, gauzy thing that did nothing to hold back the chill of December.

On the opposite side of the street, there it glowed, its bright red neon pulsing against the dark sky:

Ruby's Place.

THREE

RUSS'S PHONE woke him. The ring, not the alarm. Which was a bit odd. Who still called anyone? Called and not texted?

He pulled his head out from the hood he had made of the floral patterned comforter and tugged the phone off the nightstand. Greeted the caller with some sort of "Huhhhumoo."

The woman on the other end stuttered apologetically. Finally got herself together enough to say, "Carol's gone."

"Who?"

"Carol. The dog? Who was lost and then found?"

"Ah, the story!" Russ tried to blink his eyes into focus. "I'm not late, am I?"

"No, no, you're not. But we're not going to be able to do it after all. Carol got out of the backyard first thing. She's never been this much of an escape artist. I don't know what's gotten into her. Naughty little sprite."

"She couldn't have been gone long, though, right?" Russ tried.

"No, probably not," Scott's mother admitted. Why couldn't Russ remember her name? He could remember Aunt Joy, whose backyard had been the scene of the first escape. He guessed it was because she kept referring to herself as Scott's mother. Or maybe because it wasn't Christmas-related. Her name needed to be Mary. Or Hope. He'd be able to remember it then. "But I can't drag you all the way out here if she's missing again," she went on. "I just wouldn't feel right about that."

Russ twisted his face into a frown. He should have gotten right back on the road last night. Pressed forward. Carol had been home last night.

He thanked Scott's mom for calling and he wished her well with the search. And then he dialed another number.

"Matthews," came the answer.

"Who was the tip from?" Russ asked.

"You're in Sullivan, I'm assuming?"

"Yes."

"Sullivan Inn have some nice accommodations?"

"I can smell muffins and bacon."

"You're welcome."

"So," Russ said. "The tip?"

"Dunno," Matthews admitted.

"You sent me out here on an anonymous tip?" Russ asked, throwing the blankets off. Ten seconds ago, the idea of having to pull himself out from the warm cocoon of his bed to face a room with frosted-over windows was about as appealing as one of those January polar plunges in the nearest lake. But this admission of Matthews's was quite the cold shock in itself, frankly. The room was nothing compared to this.

"It was signed 'R.'"

"You didn't vet it?" Russ asked. "You didn't bother to try to track down who 'R' was?" He couldn't believe it. Matthews had never done anything quite so unprofessional.

"Look, it's a rumor. Basic Google skills verify rumors. What else do you need? Do a few interviews to fill up your day and tonight you go to Ruby's Place and you whip up a story and you send it my way in time for the Christmas morning edition. We had this discussion already. You're the only one I trust to turn it into something coherent and moving and tear-jerking and whatever-else-jerking on such a tight deadline. Right?"

Russ's sigh hit the cell's microphone and rattled back into his ear. "Fine. R. I'm on it." And ended the call before his disgust could make Matthews decide to go ahead and demote him to pet obituaries after all.

He dressed. Downstairs, he was greeted by a plate of over-easy eggs and cranberry orange waffles with butter and syrup. His jaw clenched at the sight of the plate. How long had it been sitting out this way? Nothing was worse than a cooling fried egg sitting on a congealed puddle of grease. Except for maybe a waffle that had been covered with syrup long enough that it was all soggy.

"Go on, go on," the innkeeper called. "Eat up!" Again, his heart lurched out toward her, inexplicably. He wanted to show her he enjoyed the breakfast, was thankful for the time she'd spent cooking for him. Why was he so strangely protective of the feelings of someone he did not know?

He smiled, pulling his chair back. Oddly, the table for two was placed in the middle of the lobby. (Had it been there the day before? Russ didn't think so.) And only one side of the table had a chair. Seemed a purposeful arrangement by the innkeeper. The absence of a chair on the other side of the table would not make him feel ill at ease about being alone on Christmas Eve.

She, oddly, seemed protective of Russ as well.

He could feel her eyes on him as he lifted his fork. He clenched his jaw as he reached for his coffee cup with his other hand. He would take a mushy, sludge-coated bite of waffle and immediately wash it down with cold coffee.

But the morsel on his mouth was hot and sweet

with an actual crispy edge. The butter was only just bare-ly melted, and the syrup was even warm. He glanced down at the coffee cup to find it steaming. He forked a bit of the egg and then stabbed another bite of waffle, running it through the syrup, all salty and sweet.

"Good?" the innkeeper asked, leaning over the front counter, her cheeks flushed. She was dressed that morning in a new sweater vest decorated with plenty of holiday-themed appliqués.

"Are these fresh cranberries?" he asked, the food muffling his voice.

"*Candied* cranberries," she corrected.

"By you?"

She let out a small squeal, clasped her hands to-gether and offered a bouncy, quick shrug.

"It's incredible. Really. And brûléed orange zest in this whipped cream, yes?"

"It was nothing. I was just so happy to have some-one to share it with. That's my own smoked bacon."

"Your own?" Russ asked, still shoveling the food. How could he be this hungry? Had he forgotten dinner last night? "You smoke it yourself?"

"When you have so much time on your hands, you find all sorts of ways to fill it."

"But doesn't the inn keep you busy?" Russ asked. He sipped the coffee. Strong and thick but not bitter. Even better than the percolator coffee in the newsroom. And just a dash of cream, no sugar. He thought about asking how she knew.

But the innkeeper confessed, "I have so few guests. Most of the time, if they're here, people don't have time to linger about. They're always just passing me by."

Russ looked down at his plate for another bite and found a second waffle. Hadn't there been one when he started? He paused, mid-bite, finding his coffee cup full again. Had a server been out to his table and given him refills in the moment he'd looked away, at the innkeeper?

"I thought for sure there would be more," the innkeeper admitted. "People who needed to stop a minute, catch their breath, find their way. But by the time they're here, they understand everything."

"What do you—" Russ tried.

"Like I said, when you have so much time on your hands, you do have the opportunity to get good at a lot of things. Like cooking." She giggled as she disappeared through a door behind the counter.

Had the door been there the night before? In the midst of the sea of keys?

Russ shook his head at himself. He'd been so thrown by this whole thing—by being sent up here by Matthews—that his mind was playing tricks on him. Why wouldn't it? Here, of all places.

He finished his breakfast. He hadn't been so full in ages. Mostly, he ate walking meals. A sandwich grabbed here, a slice of pizza there. It struck him that the last time he'd actually sat down for a meal outside of his own place was with Josie.

In six years, though? How could that be?

He fished a pen from his pocket and scribbled a note on the old-fashioned small spiral notebook that he kept with him at all times: *Thank you!* He tore out the page and left it between his empty coffee cup and the small vase with the pine sprig.

And then, without warning, he was out on the street. Snow in his eyelashes. He could not remember gathering his coat or slipping out the door. But there he was, off to try to collect some sort of story about Ruby's Place. No avoiding it now. No trying to find something else. It was too late for all of that.

As he walked, the cold air flapping his wool overcoat about his sides, he tried to figure out the feeling that had invaded him. It certainly wasn't dread. But it certainly wasn't excitement, either.

The street had a funny smell. Like cologne and exhaust and snow and candy all mixed together. The sidewalk was packed. Bustling, that was a better holiday word. Packages rustled and accidentally whacked against his calf. Heels clicked on the sidewalk. One woman waiting at a crosswalk hummed "Silver Bells."

Car trunks popped opened and names floated on the air.

It was the name thing that struck Russ, mostly. The fact that everyone knew each other. Russ didn't know any of his own neighbors' names. He didn't know Matthews's first name. With the exception of Jim in sports and that new girl, Patricia, he didn't know any of the names of the people who worked beside him in the newsroom.

What was wrong with him? How could he have become so calloused?

Even as he asked himself, he knew. A thick scab had formed over the hurt of losing Josie. The kind of scab that nothing else got through.

Funny thing about scabs, though. It worked a bit like a lid, of sorts. A seal. And the hurt of losing Josie had never slipped out, either. It was with him, like the Christmas season all those years ago. He slipped his hand into his pocket, squeezed the hair clip until it popped open.

A cardinal swooped down from a light pole and landed on the bottom ledge of a large display window.

Russ stared at it, all puffed up against the cold.

And then he shifted his gaze to the display behind him. Books, in a pyramid. *The Always Story - A Ruby's Place Tale* by Geena Barister.

He stood there, staring at the books, the reflections of passersby washing over the window, back and forth. The bell rang on the entrance of the bookstore. The Page Turner, the sign proclaimed.

A stream of shoppers exited.

Before the door fell shut, Russ slipped inside.

A man rushed back and forth behind the counter, juggling checkouts and a few piles of used books, surely brought in to exchange for Christmas gifts. A pile of business cards on the counter read, "The Page Turner - Stories Worth Repeating." Surely a nod to the *used* portion of the new and used bookstore. But somehow, at that moment, it seemed to Russ that the business card was talking directly to him, telling him that *he* was about to get hold of a story worth repeating. In print, as a matter of fact.

Because the bottom of the card read, "For store credit or to sell your collection, contact Rob at readagain@pageturner.com."

It was the first initial of the owner's name that Russ zeroed in on. R. Same as the tip.

This was it. He knew it. The story of Ruby's Place. He'd be drafting it in ten minutes. In another hour or so, he'd be driving out of Sullivan. He'd never have to open Ruby's bright green door. He'd be gone long before night fell and Christmas Eve started up, blaring through the town like an overly-loud phonograph record.

He smiled, every one of his nervous knots starting to unwind inside him. This couldn't have worked out any better.

"Can I ask about that book in the display?" Russ asked, mostly just as an ice-breaker.

"What's it like having a famous writer for a girlfriend?" chimed in another voice, this one belonging to a man standing at the counter in front of a pile of kids' books. Russ supposed he was in the process of purchasing them, the way he continued to lean over the stack.

"Don't know about famous," Rob answered. "Are any writers famous anymore?"

"It is pretty great, though. I mean, come on," the man said.

"Yeah," Rob answered. "Especially since she's wanted it so long. She was always the writer. Even during her years as a professor. And I was always the reader."

"Perfect match," Russ said, trying to insert himself, make sure the other two men didn't overlook him there.

"I thought her book was fiction," Rob said without turning away from the cash register. "But then…"

Russ's journalistic juices started to bubble. God, he loved this feeling—being right there, right at the cusp, knowing this source had it, that last key detail that would make every other detail make sense. This was going to be it. The big break. "Do you have a story you wouldn't mind sharing on the record? One about Ruby's?"

"Swore I saw my dad there one year," the man at the counter chimed in.

"No kidding?" Rob blurted, before Russ could ask him any particulars.

"Yeah, when he was alive, we used to have these nights there, you know?" the man at the counter started. "Christmas Eve, me and him. Both of us in our three-piece suits, even when I was a kid. Dad worked at the bank back then, and of course I used to imagine being just like him some day, and—"

"And now you are," Rob finished. "Working at the bank, just like him."

The man seemed a bit startled, but he softened quickly, nodding. "Yeah," he agreed.

"Still think you saw him?" Rob asked.

The man got one of those calendar expressions, the one that said he was going back in time in his mind. "Nah," he finally grumbled. "Had to have been the power of suggestion, you know? The power of memory. Maybe the power of a scotch." His cheeks flushed a light pink.

"I think I'm the only person who hasn't seen even the glimpse of someone…" Rob said. "Except one, maybe, when almost…but…" He shook his head.

"That's exactly the way it feels," the other man agreed.

"I can't figure out if I want to know the truth or want to keep the mystery," Rob said, as his cash register began to spit out a receipt.

That's why the initial only, Russ thought. *Doesn't want to commit to the tip, not entirely.*

"Sometimes mystery *is* the romance," the other man agreed.

"I ought to put that on a sign and hang it up in here somewhere," Rob said with a laugh, tugging the receipt free. He spun, facing the man as he handed the receipt to him. "But I'm not sure where I might hang it up. Mystery—"

"—or romance," they both said at the same time.

"Speaking of—you got quite a pile in," the man said, pointing.

"Yeah, a woman came in yesterday," Rob said. "Kind of a sad one."

"Needed some cash to buy gifts?"

"No, the books were sentimental, it seemed like."

"So she probably did need money," the man insisted.

"No, it was more than that," Rob said quietly. He cocked his head and crossed his arms over his chest, staring at the books in a pensive way. "Said she was letting go. That was how she put it. Like it was long past time, somehow."

Russ edged toward the counter to get a look at what the woman had brought. In the midst of the ancient, brown-spined editions were a few coffee table books. And a collection of the most influential American news photography. The spine on the photography book made his already-revved heart start to pick up the pace yet again. He could feel his scalp tighten. Goosebumps formed beneath his sleeves. He knew that spine. He had held that book before.

It couldn't be. And yet, as Russ leaned still closer, there it was—the accidental black smudge on the dust jacket. The one Josie had lamented that last Christmas. "This was in perfect shape when I bought it," she'd moaned. "I must have gotten ink on it editing." Because she'd never been able to edit on the screen. Always needed to print it out and take a pen to her work.

Russ hadn't cared. He'd loved knowing that every time he'd see the book, Josie's hand would be on it. He'd kissed her pout away.

Yes, that secondhand book on the counter of The Page Turner was definitely Russ's. The last Christmas present Josie had given him. But what was it doing here?

"That really is sad," the man at the counter agreed, as Russ started waving his hands, trying to get Rob's attention. Head swarming. Heart slamming about in the back of his throat.

"Yeah," Rob muttered. "But she sure did have the prettiest hair I've ever seen."

"Hair?" Russ muttered. "Chestnut?"

Rob pointed at the man at the counter and warned, "Don't tell Geena I said that. Noticing other women."

The man laughed, snatching up his books. "See you tonight. At Ruby's."

"See you, Scott," Rob called, and he scooped the pile of books off the counter. The same pile with Russ's book in it.

"Wait," Russ pleaded. "Wait—that—who was the woman—who?"

Josie had died six years ago. That was how it had

happened, how they'd been torn apart. At a service station on the edge of town, of all places. They had taken shelter there, with a bunch of other travelers who had raced off the highway, scrambling to get somewhere safe. They'd all huddled in the windowless back room. He could still remember the pleas and prayers and screams as the metal around them began to twist and screech.

When the tornado passed, they'd all panted, struggling to catch their breath. One man had wheezed out a few swear words and another had chuckled in relief.

Somehow, the building still stood. Mangled and warped, sure. But it stood. And so did they.

Fools that they'd been, they'd thought it was over.

And then the awful creak, like a thousand high-pitched thunderbolts. And his hand clamped on Josie's wrist, tugging. There had been a streak of light, he remembered. He'd pushed through the debris. He was the stronger of the two of them, so it was right for him to forge the way. His hand tightened and he started pulling her out of the building, right behind him.

But not fast enough.

The building had collapsed. Just like that. Who knew a metal building could flop down like that, all at once, a regular house of cards?

And there he'd been, standing in the parking lot with the few who had escaped, all of them too shocked to speak, and the air filled with the tapping sound of the rain on the twisted metal fragments of walls.

No more voices. No more pleas.

Russ was reliving all of that as Rob carried the book away. It was just a book, and yet, it felt like Josie being carried away, all over again.

Russ felt wobbly. His eyes blurred. He reached for the counter to steady himself.

The world was a smear. The kind of thing you saw on the other side of a car window when you weren't driving, when you could just mindlessly let the world speed by.

Of course he felt out of sorts, he tried to tell himself. He was in Sullivan and it was Christmas Eve and Ruby's Place would open in a few hours and this was the last place he ever wanted to be and now there was this awful story, this lie about being able to meet up with people who had died and finally telling them everything you hadn't been able to. Yes, he was here in Sullivan, trying to find some thread to tug on, some tiny little sentence that would lead to the appropriate kind of tear-jerker, all so he could get out of town before nightfall. Of course that was messing with his head, or so he tried to tell himself.

But the truth was, a part of him—a big part, the biggest part—didn't want to run at all. He wanted to be in Sullivan all Christmas Eve long. Everything in him wanted this story about Ruby's Place to be true, just like he suspected he would. He wanted to see Josie and touch her hair and give her that mother of pearl clip back. He wanted to tell her how much he loved her, even then, all those years later. She had not faded.

But the book. How could Rob have his book? How could he have seen Josie? Was Russ only wishing all of this into being? Oh, Josie. He was utterly consumed with her, even as he tried to push her out of his mind. She just kept seeping through, like water through a crack.

His ears filled with the sounds of a fast-paced clicking.

A little dog emerged from behind one of the store-length shelves, scurrying across the bookstore, toenails tapping against the tile floor. Tongue sticking out, flapping a bit with each bouncy step.

A pug. With one eye.

"Carol?" Russ called, his voice sounding like it was underwater.

The dog raced faster, straight toward the exit, just like the escape artist that her owner had claimed her to be. What was the phrase? *Naughty little sprite.*

Russ followed the jingling sound of the open door.

On the sidewalk, cold air struck him in the face. Pine garlands surrounded store entrances and red felt bows rippled in the December wind. Trying to catch his breath, he noted a distinct cinnamon smell in the air.

Pastry, maybe? Was that what had drawn the dog's attention?

There she was. Shimmying down the sidewalk in the exact direction of a bakery. Carol the missing pug.

"Wait," he called. "Wait." As though a dog ever responded to such a command. Especially from a stranger.

"Can you stop that dog?" Russ shouted, trying to appeal to the people flooding the walk.

But no one listened. Where was that small-town charm? Why was everyone simply ignoring him?

"Please," he tried again.

"Don't you worry, son," came a call from the middle of the street.

Russ turned to find a man in a three-piece suit, oversized lapels, and large sideburns halfway through the crosswalk. Waving at him. It *was* Russ he was waving at, wasn't it? As though they knew each other? But Russ had never seen this man before. Not once.

"She's going to the bank," the man explained as he stepped out of the street, patting Russ on the arm. "Carol, I mean. As soon as she gets her biscuit. This time of year, there's always someone there who remembers she liked apple cinnamon bacon bites. Made just for her."

"The—bank?" Out of everything that was just said to Russ, somehow, that was the word he'd chosen to repeat.

"She's my little helper at the bank. Carol. Has been since my son got a little older. You know how it is. The boy wants a dog, you get him one, and then the boy grows and discovers sports and girls and *you're* the one with the dog."

"So you work at the bank?"

"Oh, I retired years ago, son. Years and years. My boy works there now."

"The dog is still alive and your son is old enough now to work at the bank? Wait. Didn't you just say the dog helped *you* at the bank?"

The man eyed him in a way that said he was surprised Russ knew so little. "Aren't you staying at The Sullivan Inn?"

"Yes."

"Oh. Well. I thought our innkeeper might have explained a little more."

"What do you mean?"

"I have but one job at the bank these days. I'm in charge of the vault."

"The vault."

"That's where the memory bank is, son. The one I have to open up each Christmas Eve."

"Memory bank?"

"Well, son, there wouldn't be a Ruby's Place without memories, now would there?"

"I don't understand."

The man put his fingers in his mouth and whistled, unleashing such a horrible high-pitched screech that Russ cringed and took a step away from him. No one else on the street so much as flinched, though. Not a

48

single hiccup in their step.

"There she is," the man said, pointing at the pug scurrying in the opposite direction now, on the other side of the road. "Finished with her treat. Better hurry myself. No one else at the bank will let her in."

"I didn't get your name." Russ blurted the old reporter's question because he was trying to hold on to this man, get him to explain.

"Walter," he said. "Walter Drummond."

"And your son? At the bank?"

"Scott," he offered, finding no strangeness in being asked about him.

"But that's the name of the boy in my, my…story."

"Always did regret that name when he was younger," Walter admitted. "If I'd known he would have such a bad stutter as a boy, I would have named him something else. The 's' at the beginning, followed by the hard consonant and the 't' at the end…just a minefield for the poor boy, anytime someone asked his name. Such a hard way to start any conversation. Answer any teacher's question."

"A stutter?" Russ repeated.

But Walter was already back in the crosswalk, waving to the pug. "Carol! Come on, old girl. We've got a job to do."

"What? What?" Russ asked. Hadn't the man inside the bookstore been Scott? Hadn't he and Rob said he worked at the bank, like his dad? Hadn't he implied he had himself seen his own father in Ruby's Place after his father had died? And what about the one-eyed pug named Carol? The one Russ had found on Facebook who had just gotten back to a young Scott? Precious Carol, who helped Scott relax and not stutter?

Was that the same Carol? How could she have escaped her yard in another town that morning, and then already be in Sullivan? How could her owner be here, too? How could Scott suddenly be a grown man?

Russ pulled his phone from his pocket, but he could find no messages between himself and Scott's mother. No texts. No record of her call that morning.

He shook his head, confused. What was going on? Had he been so desperate to avoid Sullivan that he had made the whole thing with the dog up? How did that make sense, considering he had just seen Carol himself a moment ago?

He thought about going back inside the bookstore. Buying one of the copies of the book, at least. The ones on display, the ones by Rob's girlfriend. The Ruby's Place books. Surely there was something in it. While he was there, he could ask Rob about the man he had spoken to, and who Walter was, and if he knew anything about a memory bank.

But when he turned back toward that window, there they were all over again, reflected in the glass: the passersby, racing to get their last-minute Christmas errands done.

Russ's reflection was not there.

He let out a strangled kind of yelp and raced away from the window. There was no logic here. Not in any of this. Not in the perfect breakfast with the just-in-time miraculously appearing second waffle, or the way Russ had wound up in Sullivan despite his best efforts not to, or even in Matthews suddenly deciding to run some schmaltzy Christmas Day piece or decorate his office, turning old typewriter ribbon into tinsel. Everything felt upside-down.

Russ raced away, down the street. He would go to the bank. He needed to talk to Walter. That was better than talking to Rob.

That bakery smell found him again. Cinnamon. But, no, not quite. Almost musky, really. Like women's cologne. The kind that Josie had preferred, because she hadn't liked to smell like a bunch of flowers.

In fact, it *was* Josie's perfume. His feet kept moving forward, but he was spinning.

And then he was stumbling, and time suddenly turned slow-motion, like it had a tendency to do sometimes right before something awful happened. Two seconds stretched into ten minutes. He was falling, and all he could think was that he was about to hit the sidewalk. Spend the holiday in the Sullivan hospital.

Instead of crashing into the pavement, he landed in someone's arms. He didn't really feel caught, though.

How could he? The arms that had kept him from disaster were rough and hard, and they were as cold as December.

FOUR

"Josie?" HE ACTUALLY SAID her name out loud. But the arms beneath him weren't covered in the soft suede of Josie's favorite winter coat. And they didn't immediately wrap around him and squeeze, like Josie's always had. The arms he had stumbled into were made of concrete. They were dotted with snow and ice. And they belonged to a cluster of sculptures outside of the Sullivan library. Readers of all ages, each one of them with frozen smiles on their faces and books in their hands.

Russ backed up, away from the statues. Something about the look of them unnerved him. Instead of seeming playful and fun, they seemed more like stone figures in a cemetery.

It didn't help that night had somehow fallen. That the sculptures were cloaked in a kind of blue-tinged moonlight.

How was this possible, though? Hadn't Russ just had breakfast? Had he somehow lost time?

He eyed the sculpture of the woman sitting cross-legged, a giant edition spread across her lap. His thoughts zipped straight back to his own coffee table book, the one he had just seen in The Page Turner. Or had it been hours ago? Where had the rest of the day gone?

He rubbed his forehead, trying to think. He was certain he had not given that book up. Not that one. He hadn't seen it in ages, but that was only because he had put it away, somewhere out of sight. Nothing eye level, where memories would constantly be finding him. But where? On top of the bookcase? A bottom shelf, one of the ones obscured by his reading chair? Why couldn't he picture it? All he knew, right then, was that it was an object with too much weight attached to it. The kind of thing that Russ would have always found impossible to look at or give away.

And yet, he had also been surprised at finding Josie's hair clip the day before. Had grief mixed every-thing up in his mind—what he had kept, what he had donated? Why was nothing quite clear anymore? Noth-ing but the memory of that last Christmas Eve, the two of them sitting in his car, heat pouring from the dashboard, the stars on the other side of the windshield. "Who wants to wait for tomorrow?" Josie had asked, handing him his gift. "It's Christmas Eve. Perfect time for shredding some wrapping paper."

It had clearly been a book, even before Russ had unwrapped it. Unmistakable—the size of it, the feel of it in his hand. Maybe an impersonal gift to anyone else, but with Josie, it was a sign that they understood each other like no other. They were the same.

He simply could not fathom the possibility that he had given it up. Why would he do that? Knowing that it would wind up somewhere like The Page Turner, in Sullivan, of all places? Why would he allow it to become a meaningless object left for some stranger to pick up and turn over in their hands and then decide it really wasn't worth ten bucks after all? Never. It wasn't just a book. It was one of the very last moments he had spent with Josie.

Russ stumbled up the stone stairs, toward the building's entrance, not really sure what he wanted with a library. Just to sit down a minute, maybe. Get inside somewhere, away from the cold. That was it. He needed a minute to catch his breath.

Inside, the library smelled of pine. He thought he could barely make out the sounds of some sort of workers' holiday party. Polite laughter, the kind of animated chatter that normally no one would dare allow to disturb a library.

Christmas attacked him once again. The same Christmas he had wanted to evade in the newsroom, before ever being given this assignment. He could hear a distant carol and a soft jingling noise. In front of him, in the half-darkened library, twinkled a giant tinsel-wrapped tree meant to welcome library patrons.

Russ turned one corner, then another. How could he have so quickly lost the direction back to the main entrance? He needed to get out of there. He did not want this. He did not want any more Christmas. Not for him.

Christmas was for people who were good. That much had been driven into him since he was a little boy. Gifts for the good, coal for those who had misbehaved. Naughty and nice lists.

What did he deserve? What did any man deserve who let a woman like Josie slip out of his grasp, just as the rest of the tornado-weakened building around them collapsed?

He deserved nothing. No gifts, no love, no happiness.

Certainly not Christmas. Never again.

His shin whacked something hard and sharp. He grunted, touched his leg, expecting to find a goose egg already bulging up underneath his pants.

No such swelling, though. He clearly hadn't hit it quite as hard as he'd thought.

A metal drawer there in the research island in the

center of the library had clearly been the culprit. Pulled out, sticking in the way of anyone trying to walk by, exposing the rolls of microfilm inside. His hand was suddenly fishing one roll out, even though he didn't think he'd decided to. But it was the right date. Six years ago. And he was feeding it into a reader, and inexplicably, he was zipping straight to the coverage of that Christmas. The last one.

There it was. Front page. The story of the storm. The building collapse. That horrible picture, the pile of wreckage mirroring exactly what Russ's heart had become.

He could not read the details. But he looked at the byline:

Josie Palmer.

"What?" he hissed, ready to argue with the type right there on the screen.

He glanced about, hoping someone was nearby to *shhh* him. That someone could have told him what they saw on the screen.

But there was no one.

Russ leaned closer. The byline remained.

That wasn't right. This couldn't be. Josie didn't write this story. Josie was already gone by the time the Christmas morning edition hit newsstands and front porches.

He had written the story. Russ Keegan. That was the right byline. How could Josie's name be there instead?

He twisted the zoom dial until the byline filled the entire screen.

Josie Palmer.

Something was very wrong.

He pushed himself away from the microfilm reader. Somehow, without walking through the door or passing by the concrete sculptures, he was back out on the street, the sounds of the Christmas he did not deserve all around him. Josie's cologne filled his nose. Doors jingled open. Packages crinkled. Something was missing. Josie, of course, but something else, too.

Maybe it was a part of himself. Maybe that was the missing piece.

Russ felt as though all these details surrounding his Sullivan trip were made of sentences spoken in a foreign language. Random sounds that didn't translate and only confused him even more. Snow was getting heavier. Obscuring everything.

Across the street, the bright red neon of the Ruby's Place sign glowed warm as a stove burner against the night sky. Like something dangerous, something that could hurt him if he got too close.

The bright green front door swung open over and again.

Ahead of him, Russ recognized the same long chestnut locks he had once known so well. There they went, on the opposite side of the street, rippling off the back of a woman's shoulders in the December wind.

Josie? Could it be? Was she still here, haunting the last place she had been happy? Was she trying to get his attention?

Did she know? Did she understand all of it? The inexplicable timeline with the dog, the strange man from the bank? Could she explain the byline?

Mindlessly, Russ staggered into the middle of the street.

Just as a car turned the corner.

He gasped, jerked, lunged out of the way.

But the car sped along without a squeal of the brakes or so much as a honk.

Had they not seen him in all this foot traffic? How could they not have?

Ahead of him, the chestnut locks disappeared behind the bright green Ruby's Place door.

And he knew: it really was true, that story about Ruby's Place. It wasn't a Christmas Eve rumor. It wasn't schmaltz. Spirits really did fill Ruby's Place on Christmas Eve.

Russ was moving, but not staggering. Not anymore.

He was walking. And he was moving directly toward the one place he'd once sworn he'd never enter. Not ever again.

FIVE

RUSS STOPPED JUST SHY of stepping inside. Christmas Eve revelers streamed around him, laughing happily as they threw open the bright green Ruby's Place door. Really threw it, with everything they had, not seeming to care if they accidentally bumped into him.

Was he actually going inside? Why? What would he do there? What if the hair he saw was on a different person entirely? Did he plan on asking someone at the bar if they could also smell the love of his life's perfume?

This was stupid. Had he really been ready to believe, a few seconds ago, that he could talk to Josie? What was wrong with him?

He could not get a grip on the world, suddenly.

But something in him refused to retreat. Maybe only his reporter's need to push on, get to the end of the story.

An old woman sat on a bench beside the Ruby's Place entrance, wearing a coat the same color as the bench's holiday-red paint. Just sitting there, as the snow collected on her shoulders and the empty bench beside her.

A river of Sullivanites scurried right past her, not caring that they were bumping into her leg or whacking her face with the flap of a coat. It was all quite similar to the way those trying to get inside Ruby's had just treated him.

Why? Because they were both outsiders, maybe? Russ wasn't quite sure why he latched onto the possibility, only knew there had to be something connecting the two of them.

Did this woman have the look of having come from another town? What, exactly, did an out-of-towner even look like? How was any one person any different from another?

Maybe he and the old woman were simply unrecognizable faces. No one knew their names, and that made them easy to ignore?

For the tiniest of moments, Russ considered the idea that he and the old woman were both somehow invisible. An impossibility, but then again, so was everything that had been happening to him for the last twenty-four hours.

At any rate, it was the first time in ages that he saw another person and thought, *Hey, you. Here we are together, you and me.*

"Have you been here before?" he asked.

She turned to face him, and for a moment, he was afraid of what he had stepped into. Was that a Christmas reverie on her face, or was she shriveling inside? How old was she, really? Wasn't it odd that she was sitting out here in the freezing cold, barely thirty degrees? Sitting so long that a good half-inch of flakes had gathered on the shoulders of her red wool coat?

Maybe, he thought, his eyes drifting toward the large plate glass window, someone was inside looking for her, not seeing her anywhere, and starting to get a little panicked.

But she smiled at him, and there was a sharpness in it. The kind of sharpness that told him she knew exactly what she was doing.

"Quite the night, isn't it?" she asked. "A sight that can't be taken in all in one blink," she went on, making it sound perfectly reasonable that she would be sitting outside in the freezing cold.

She nodded toward the square lined with businesses and crowded with cars and voices and bright bulging Christmas packages tucked under arms. And somehow, in that instant, none of it seemed plastic or cheap or forced. It didn't seem empty or like a desperate sales pitch. It seemed…why, it seemed to sparkle there a moment. The same way Christmas had sparkled in the years before Russ had ever learned how truly deep heartache could slice. A sense of calm found him. The kind of calm that could make space for anticipation. That flutter in the stomach of excitement.

And in that moment, it all made sense. Why *wouldn't* the woman be out here, taking it all in? The landscape before them was not just decorated. Festooned. That was more like it. Somehow, standing here, his eyes shifting between the street and the twinkle in the woman's eyes, even the tinsel began to look less tacky and more like a promise intended to be kept. The sounds of laughter and carols and piano chords bled through the bricks of Ruby's Place, and the melody insisted that it was the non-believer—anyone who did *not* recognize the magic of the night or accept the myth of Santa with all their heart—who was the fool.

"Have you?" Russ asked, returning to his original question. "Have you been here before?" He sensed she knew things. Like maybe he could even tell her about everything that had happened to him that morning, and she could help him.

"Every Christmas Eve. Long as I can remember," she said, smiling wistfully. So she wasn't a stranger to Sullivan after all.

"I'm Russ," he tried, extending a hand.

"You're a newspaperman," she corrected in a rather distrustful tone.

How could she have known? And why could that be a bad thing?

"I'm not—I mean," Russ blubbered. "I *am*, I'm a reporter. But I'm not here as one tonight." Such a lie. Only, in that moment, it didn't feel like one.

Why, though? He was not here to see Josie. He knew better than that, he reminded himself as he reached into his pocket to squeeze the hair clip.

"A reporter is always a reporter. You don't turn that off," she argued.

"Are you telling me there really is a story in there?" Russ asked, pointing to the building behind her. "One that I'm going to want to write?"

She only offered a knowing smirk.

"It's silly, really," Russ said, afraid of the knowledge in her grin. "The holiday got to me," he added, backing up. "I shouldn't have bothered you. I'm sorry. You have a good Christmas, ma'am."

He couldn't go in. He didn't care about Matthews, or how angry he would be. He could fire him if he had to. That was how much Russ needed to get out of there.

"You've heard about Christmas Eve, haven't you?" she called out to him, her voice racing to reach him before he was out of earshot. "And how, on that one night a year, you can—well. You can speak to the dead."

Russ stopped. And he retreated, against his own

will. "That's kind of a *not* Christmasy way of saying it," he said, deciding to stand a little closer this time.

"But that's what they say."

"Yes," he agreed, his mind drifting off toward the vision he had seen walk through the door of Ruby's, "that's what they say."

"There's someone you would like to see," the woman said. "Someone you have gotten all your hopes up to see. Someone you would like to see so badly, it might destroy you if you walked inside and you *didn't* see them."

And there it was: the truth. The fear and the terror and the hope. All the things he wanted to say to Josie, and all the things he was afraid she would say in return.

"Yeah," he admitted, his voice lower, getting that funny sound that revealed tears threatened to make their way in. "Yeah, there's someone I would like to see."

The woman picked a cocktail up off the bench beside her. Had it always been there, though? Russ could have sworn the bench had been empty as he'd approached her for the first time.

"The thing about magic," the woman said, "is that it isn't a thing all on its own." She gripped her swizzle stick in such a way that she left her pinky extended. "It doesn't show up without asking. It doesn't *volunteer* itself."

"No?"

"It's made of ingredients."

Russ almost didn't hear that last part. Her voice sounded funny suddenly. Tinny. Almost melodic and old-fashioned. Like a music box in an antique store.

But he shrugged it off. Probably, her voice hit the edge of her cocktail glass. Kind of like how a wet fingertip could make that funny ringing sound when it circled the rim.

"Are you an ingredient?" Russ asked.

The woman smiled, leaned back against the bench. "*You* are," she said.

Six

Russ staggered into the building, mostly to get away from the old woman. The reporter in him knew that he needed to stay, ask what she'd meant by that ingredient statement. But the still-grieving man in him, the same one who had lost Josie and spent the past six years trying to avoid feeling anything that deep for anyone else, stumbled across the floor of the supper club.

He had only come through the door to get away from her. But that meant he was now inside, the unmistakable smell of toasted marshmallows in his nose. He spun. Surely there had to be another way out. A back door.

Wasn't that the big story about Ruby's? That it had once been a speakeasy? That there was an alleyway, a back entrance where patrons had once rapped out a secret knock, whispered a password?

No one had ever wanted in as much as Russ wanted out at that very moment.

But the crowds had already descended on Ruby's. Now that he was inside, the crush of bodies just kept forcing him in deeper, prevented him from looking for another exit. The place was full, maybe even more so than it had been on that fateful night six years ago. Shouting and laughing and cheers exploding with each arrival, each swing of the door. And then more bodies, making for a still-tighter squeeze. An old upright piano along a far wall had attracted a large group, all in a semi-circle, their arms making a kind of daisy chain around shoulders, swaying back and forth together, singing in unison.

And everyone was so dressed up. To the nines, that would have been the phrase that would have been tossed out years ago. Jewelry and cashmere, freshly-ironed dresses, and stockings and heels. Painted nails and red lipstick. Suits and crisp white shirts. Cufflinks. Who wore cufflinks anymore? Dress shoes. Ties.

Russ found himself pushed across the floor by the tide of revelers. Looking for something to brace himself, he gripped the edge of the bar. The wood beneath his fingers felt polished by all the touches that had come before, like something warm and comfortable and oddly thrilling—the skin on the arm of a love you'd had for years.

It came back to him how he and Josie had admired the bar, running their hands along the ornate details. Enormous and thick and heavy, and also carved with flowers and leaves, each of them recreated down to the tiniest element. Each acanthus leaf had a vein and folds and one flower even had a lady bug on it. Josie had said it seemed like a trinket box for a giant.

He had laughed at Josie's way of seeing the world.

And now, all these years later, he was gripping the same bar, trying to stay upright.

A glass slid under his nose, the contents sloshing a bit over the rim and splashing his hand.

"This isn't mine. I didn't order anything," he insisted, trying to push it back. The glass was cold against his fingers, making him realize just how hot he'd gotten inside the club, as though he'd already spent an hour inside Ruby's.

"It's just ice water," explained the bartender, a middle-aged woman, slender body like an illustration from an old art nouveau poster. Sinewy, that was maybe the right word. Dark hair twisted into a bun on the back of her head. Her white silk blouse shimmered a little, like it had golden threads woven through it.

"Thanks," he breathed, sliding onto a stool. "Quite the crowd tonight."

"It's Christmas Eve," she said, shrugging.

This, Russ thought, was the perfect opening. "I'm on assignment," he admitted. Even though he'd promised the woman outside he wasn't. He shouldn't have lied to her. He twisted on the stool, angling toward the door, as though he could see her through the plate glass. But there were too many patrons blocking his view. He remembered the cocktail that had appeared in her hand and thought surely the bartender had served her.

"Do you know the old woman sitting outside?" he asked. "The one on the bench?"

"Hetty," she said.

"Is she senile?"

"Hardly."

"She said I was an ingredient."

The bartender offered only the slightest hint of a smile. "She's right."

"She's right?"

"She *is* the resident expert on magic. Well, magic and music boxes."

Russ remembered the strange tone in the woman's voice—the high-pitched, tinny twang. He had thought that very term: music box. He must have been looking at the bartender with utter confusion, because she explained, "You need music to trigger memories, right? Christmas is the season of memories. And her husband used to make music boxes."

"When was that?" Russ asked. He reached into

his coat, pulled out his small notebook and clicked his pen. All he had to do was snag a few quotes from the bartender, snap a picture of her (and as nice as she looked, dressed for the holiday with a glass poinsettia pin and matching red lipstick, she would absolutely be open to having her picture taken), and then he'd be on his way. No need to get lost in his own past, in the last time he was here with his Josie.

And he certainly wouldn't have to uselessly glance about, over and over, only to realize the chestnut hair he thought he'd seen had been wishful thinking. He would not have to be reminded that Josie was still nowhere.

Just as Josie had been nowhere for exactly six years.

"Oh, about a hundred years ago," the bartender said.

"Hetty's husband sold music boxes a hundred years ago."

"More or less," she said.

Before Russ could figure out how to make his mouth work, the bartender was already slipping away, heading for the kitchen. Russ feared she would simply disappear into her work, assuming he was taken care of for a while. There he'd be, stuck just blowing time there at the bar. What was he going to do, stare at his melting cubes until she could work her way back?

What could she have meant by that? A hundred years ago? Surely that was hyperbole. Or a joke. The bartender was just saying that because the woman seemed so old. It had nothing to do with the whole story about spirits at Ruby's Place on Christmas Eve. It couldn't.

Then again, the entire town had seemed strange upon his arrival. The bookstore. The innkeeper. The pug that had somehow traveled twenty-plus miles in a single morning. His missing reflection in the front of the bookstore, the plate glass window showing all the other townspeople racing up and down the sidewalk but not him.

The byline.

As his confusion gave way to fear, Russ told himself to focus. To get control of himself. Work on his story. That was the only way to make sense of it all. Dig deeper, get to the bottom of it all. The truth was always there, at the bottom.

He needed to get that bartender's attention. He raised his hand, index finger extended. But she didn't notice.

As he watched her through the window in the kitchen door, he caught himself thinking how she moved like the cattails along the edge of the lake where he and Josie and once vacationed. All that gentle swaying back and forth in the breeze as he and Josie had sat on their dock, watching sunsets.

It was a dancer's grace, he thought, that's what the bartender had. At first, that simple thought pleased him. But as the word settled inside him—*dancer*, like an ice cube drifting to the bottom of a glass—he turned prickly all over.

What was happening to him? A logical, fact-driven journalist? He couldn't actually be considering it, could he?

Even as he told himself not to, his eyes were darting up to where he knew he would find pictures behind the bar. Images of all the different women who had been part of the building's past. There she was: Frankie, who had run both a respectable diner ("Home of the 5¢ steak!") and a speakeasy. (Yes, yes, he remembered now, he'd been right. This place *had* been a speakeasy, accessible after dark with a secret knock at the alley door.) And there, in another slightly-faded photograph, why, that was Dorothy leaning against the piano, the jazz singer in her charmeuse gown with her flapper hair and the gardenia behind her ear. The same Dorothy who had performed at the speakeasy alongside her trumpeter husband. And to the far right of both hung the photo of Ruby herself, who had bought the place and turned it into a supper club in the 1950s once her career as a ballerina had run out.

Ruby Westbrook. Forever preserved in that photo wearing a white silk blouse. And a poinsettia brooch. Her dark hair tied into a ballerina bun at the back of her head.

Just like that bartender?

Russ frowned, craning his neck to look into the

kitchen. He thought he could hear the bartender's voice, but he couldn't see her. He waved at one of the cooks, trying to flag her attention, but it didn't work.

Impatience kicked Russ right in the ribs. He wanted to shout. He needed to talk to someone. Answers didn't show up all on their own.

Surely there was someone.

A woman in an awful brown knit hat, cheeks flushed from the heat of the overflowing crowd, passed by him on the other side of the bar, an empty pitcher in her hand.

"I think I know you," he said. Blurted it before he could stop himself, refine his approach.

The woman snorted a surprised laugh.

Russ pointed at her, his eyebrows tenting. "Angela!"

She laughed again. She had a nice laugh. An honest one, the kind that said the person attached to it had never, not once in her life, simply laughed to be polite.

"That's me, all right," she said.

"I can remember because it's a little Christmasy, what with the 'angel' in it, and I…" Russ stopped. It was almost too hard to say.

"…and the last time you were here, it was Christmas," Angela predicted.

"Right. And you, you're the current owner. So you told…us." That last word, that *us,* was quite nearly unbearable. That single syllable sent Russ spiraling, his mind tumbling back into the past, to a Christmas six years gone, when Angela had leaned against the bar and told Russ and Josie all about the women in the photos behind the bar. Journalists liked their facts and dates, and Angela had been more than happy to rattle them off the top of her head, serving them up to be savored alongside the marshmallows.

"How do you know so much about the place?" Josie'd asked, taking another sip of her hot cocoa. "Seems more intimate than just learning about a building after you bought it."

God, Russ had loved her in that moment. It was always his favorite thing about her, that ability of hers to size up situations so accurately. Almost like x-ray vision, but for other people's hearts. Josie Palmer knew you—saw every last microscopic piece of your soul—just by looking.

"Used to come here with my aunt," Angela'd said. "Every single Christmas. Back when I was a little girl. Wound up buying the place quite some time after Ruby had passed. Decided to renovate. Put it all back the way it had been, once upon a time. Felt a little like bringing a memory to life, you know?"

"You bought this place after Ruby's death," Russ recited quietly.

Again, the laugh. "You remember well."

"*After* her death."

"Yes?" Angela cocked her head, sweat running

along her cheek.

Russ wondered, for the briefest of moments, why in the world she kept that hat on. "There's a story about this place," he said. "Have you heard it? About how, one night a year—"

"—Christmas spirits are more than just the liquors behind the bar."

"You repeat that a lot?"

"I do." Angela looked directly at him, as though these two tiny syllables should have carried an immense weight.

"You restored the place. Had to, it had been empty so long. After Ruby died."

"Right."

"So who is that in the kitchen?" Russ tried. "The one with the bun?"

But Angela was already gone. He spun around, finding her standing over by the piano, belting out a carol along with the rest of her holiday merrymakers.

Had she ever been at the bar talking to him? What was wrong with him? All these tricks his mind had been playing on him, from the minute his tires had crossed the city limits.

Maybe, this time, it was something as simple as the heat of the place getting to him? All these people, all the dancing and shouting and moving about. It was almost like being in a gym. He reached up to wipe sweat from his own brow.

76

But his fingertips came back dry.

Trembling, he picked up his water glass.

"You already know what goes on here on Christmas Eve, don't you, Russ?"

He coughed against the cold water on his tongue.

She was back. The bartender. Bun, silk shirt, red poinsettia pin.

"How did you know my name?"

"I know all about your assignment," the bartender said.

"Did Matthews call?" Russ asked.

Again with the grin. "Didn't he tell you about the tip?"

"Are *you* the 'R'?" he asked. It couldn't be, though. After taking a breath, he dared to say, "I didn't catch your name—"

"I'm Ruby." She extended a hand.

"Ruby—who?"

"Westbrook. This is my place."

"Can't be," Russ said. "You—you—"

"I what?" she asked, leaning her elbows on the bar, seeming to enjoy herself.

"You'd already died when I was here. Before. Six *years* before. Angela owned the place."

"She still does," the woman affirmed. She leaned to the side and waved at the woman still singing away at the piano.

Angela didn't seem to notice her.

"What are the Christmas spirits?" Russ asked, his voice breaking. "Are they ghosts?"

Ruby barked a laugh. "Ghosts," she repeated. "Don't you know the world's not that either-or? Isn't a memory really kind of a ghost?"

"What does any of this mean?" Russ asked, but dread was bitter in his mouth.

"It means we've been expecting you, Mr. Keegan," Ruby told him.

"Why would you—"

"I saw your editor Matthews here the other day."

Russ shook his head. "You couldn't have. He was at work. At the newsroom." He wanted to push himself from the bar. But he was stuck, somehow. Like a machine with all its moving parts rusted into place. Something hot and acidic was rising inside of him. A mere week ago, he would have called it bile.

Something in him already stopped short of using that word.

"There's a story," he said. "My editor sent me to check it out. No, not a story. A rumor."

"That in here, you can speak to the dead," Ruby whispered, her hand cupped around her mouth. She spoke in an overly animated way, widening her eyes to feign shock.

But when Russ whispered back, he was serious. "Yes."

"And Matthews sent you out here for the kind of

human interest piece you hate."

"How would you know that? That I can't stand those fluff pieces?"

"I spoke to—"

"You couldn't have," Russ insisted, slamming his fists on the bar. "Stop saying that."

Ruby cocked her head to the side and offered a look of sympathy.

"This can't be happening, Ruby," he said. But it was, because he knew she was real. Every bit as real as he was.

"It already *happened*," she said, putting a hand on his.

His ears filled with a horrible scraping noise. The sound of a chair being dragged across the floor. But no, that wasn't right. It sounded more like the building he and Josie had taken shelter in, the way it had creaked and screeched out warning sounds as the tornado had spun into their path.

He didn't understand. Or, more accurately, he didn't want to understand. Not this.

He turned his eyes away from Ruby. He needed something else to look at. Something other than her woeful expression. The mirror. That would be a safe place to put his eyes. Or so he told himself.

But for the second time that day, he did not see his reflection. He didn't see revelers or a piano or the chandelier, either. He did not see the bar.

Instead, he saw that last night with Josie. His heart wrenched inside his chest. He knew it, the look of it. He would recognize it anywhere. There they were, taking shelter inside the filling station off the highway. The lights flickering. Walls rattling and whipping about. The wind had such force, it felt alive. Hellbent on retribution, though no one knew for what.

His fingers scratched against the dim gray shadows until they found Josie's arm. They circled her wrist, tugged her ahead of him.

Watching it, fear found him again, that same fear that had engulfed him back then. He watched Josie pulling against him, and could feel her wrenching herself free. Refusing to go first. He could feel the warmth of her breath on the side of his face as she screamed at him, "Go. I'll follow you."

Already, this was wrong. That's not how he'd remembered it for the past six years. He had gone first, and there had been no protest from Josie. He had never tried to make her go ahead of him. He was stronger and it made more sense for him to clear the way.

He went first, and that was why he got out and Josie did not.

But what he watched in that mirror was his hand tightening his grip on Josie and pulling her out in front of him, even as she tried to fight him on it.

Josie went first. And then the building screeched and groaned all around him.

In the end, there she stood, on the outside. There she was, in the parking lot. Crying. Refusing to leave as the search and rescue team arrived.

"If only that had happened," Russ murmured.

"But it did."

When he pulled his eyes away, Ruby was giving him a kind of stern look that insisted he believe her. "You saw the truth up there," she said. "You got her out. Josie. You pushed her out."

"So you're saying…" Russ started. But he shook his head. That wasn't right. He was the one who'd survived. Not Josie.

Again, Ruby cocked her head and flashed her sympathetic look. "Don't you remember? Right before the tornado—before what you just watched—she was pushing open an entryway," Ruby said.

Had she?

Yes. "We had this enormous tree poking through the roof," Russ said, "one of those hundred-year-old varieties. And we had a semi there, too, blown into the front of the building from the highway. A whole…" He swallowed. "A whole semi."

"The building didn't come down with the tornado," Ruby said.

That much was right. "It didn't," Russ agreed. "But it was so mangled. The hole in the ceiling was too high up to get to and the door was all twisted, but there was another opening. It was a service station, where we were. Not just a gas station. One of those old-fashioned places that did smaller repairs on your car. So there was a jack in there. To change tires, that sort of thing."

Russ slumped on his barstool, pausing his story a moment. "I forgot about the jack. How could I do that?"

"What about the jack?" Ruby coaxed.

"Josie found it. The two of us were both pressing on it, forcing it to open up a space where everyone could squeeze out. That did work, didn't it?"

"You saved quite a few," Ruby agreed.

"We were fighting over which of the two of us would go first. When it was down to just us. When we were the last two. And the building was making this awful noise. And…"

"And what?" Ruby asked.

"She was trying to push me ahead of her. But I was, you know—" Russ licked his lips. His mouth was dry enough to burn, but he didn't dare take a sip of his drink.

"You were bigger," Ruby suggested.

"Yeah. I was bigger. I was stronger. I won the shoving war. I—"

"You did it," Ruby said. "You got her out."

"What's happening?" Russ whispered. But the byline came back to him, the most black-and-white proof in the entire situation. In a rush of sadness, he said, "I didn't get out, did I?"

Ruby's eyes held the answer.

"Is Matthews dead?" Russ asked.

"He never existed," Ruby told him.

"This makes no sense," Russ said, swiveling to look out at the rest of Ruby's Place. "I was here. Before the storm. It was real then."

"Of course it was," Ruby told him. "So was I. So were you."

"But then—"

"You exist right now because Josie remembers you. That newsroom of yours? That's where she imagined you continuing on. If you could have lived another day—another year—that's exactly where you would have wanted to be. In a newsroom full of hardcore journalists. And Matthews is the editor she dreamed up for you. He's a kind of an amalgam of—"

"—of every editor she ever had, combined with all the Lou Grants she ever saw on TV," Russ finished. Hadn't he thought something similar off and on for the last six years? That Matthews was a sitcom version of an editor?

"This life you've been living," Ruby went on, "it's the life Josie dreamed up for you because she couldn't bear the alternative."

"And the alternative is the truth," Russ said. He knew he should be crying. But he wasn't. He had no tears. "The alternative is that I'm the one who died in that filling station. Not Josie."

"Don't you see?" Ruby pressed. "Most people,

they're remembered in flashes. In snippets. Scenes from the past. Josie loved you so much she dreamed an entire life for you, beyond the one you lived."

"The story—the tale of Ruby's Place—"

"Everyone here has a memory. Do you even remember learning about Christmas for the first time?" Ruby asked. "I don't. It's like I just always knew what it was. And most of my life, I was aching to tap into some Christmas that had come before."

"Ruby's Place is a where you can tap into what was," Russ said. "The best times. Like stepping into a living photograph."

Ruby flushed, pleased. "More," she whispered. "It's more. When you are remembered, you are still alive."

"But by one person, right?"

"There are individual memories, yes. Memories of lives. But—there are bigger memories. Town-wide memories. Sometimes, those big memories are really just stories that get told. Repeated over and over."

Russ turned, his eyes darting toward the old woman outside. "Stories repeated until they become a kind of legend," he said. "Passed from one generation to the next."

"Yes," Ruby whispered.

"Angela tells them," Russ said. "She told them to us. Me and Josie. Those pictures behind the bar. The history of this place. She told us."

Ruby nodded. "She's folded so much of my own

story into hers. That's how memory works."

"Storytelling," Russ said.

"Told over and over. Repeated to keep it real," Ruby agreed. "That's what Josie's been doing for you. Repeating thoughts of you to keep you real."

"The things that didn't make sense—the gaps—the—me not remembering being on the road, or knowing Matthews's first name—"

"Gaps in Josie's storytelling," Ruby said.

"But the hair clip."

"Her fondest memory of *you*. Maybe one of your own as well. But her fondest of you. One of the things she missed the most when you were gone. Taking down her hair."

Again, the clicking of toenails.

"There," Russ said, pointing at the tiny running creature. "There. That dog. That's proof."

"That what I've told you isn't true?" Ruby asked.

"I just saw it—on Facebook. I found the post."

"I've talked to Josie plenty, you know," Ruby told him. "Every single Christmas Eve, when she returns. She's been one of my regulars. Since your last Christmas. She's talked fondly of how the two of you used to laugh about the dumb human interest pieces you were both assigned at the start of your careers."

A cold sensation crawled down his arms. "Carol the dog," Russ said. "That was Josie's story. Scott's dog. It happened years and years ago. How could I have forgotten?" But he already knew the answer: because Josie had wanted him to.

"The innkeeper?" he asked.

"Making waffles Josie knew you'd love."

"Those strange things the innkeeper said. Almost mystical. Smelling Josie's perfume on the street."

"Josie has been calling you here. So that you can meet up face to face. This Christmas Eve. Finally."

Ruby slid a plate of marshmallows beneath his nose, just like the ones he and Josie had eaten that last Christmas. "Josie said you liked them the year you came. Even though you weren't a fan of sweets."

"She said it must have been because our love had made me sweet inside," Russ said. "That the taste just complemented what was in my heart."

"And you?" Ruby asked.

"I laughed. I told her she was the one who was getting schmaltzy." Russ squinted at Ruby. "So the story of Ruby's Place, that grand myth of the spirits. Did Josie make that up, too? Is it not true for anyone else?"

"Oh, it's true," Ruby said. "For those whose memories are strong enough."

"But if I'm a memory, as you say, if my life right now is the work of her imagination, why wouldn't she have wanted me out here before this? Why wouldn't she—?"

Russ's voice trailed as he was brought back to the image of the coffee table book on the counter of The

Page Turner. His book, the one Josie had given him. And in his ears lingered the echo of the conversation, Rob talking to the other man at the counter. Never to Russ directly. Neither one of those men had heard him.

That had been Josie at work. All along. She had wanted him to see it. All of it. She had wanted him to know what he was, in a way he would accept and not question in his true reporter's way. She had to have loved keeping his memory alive, coming out each Christmas Eve, reliving the best part of their last night together. But now...

"She's letting me go, isn't she?"

Seven

For a slice of a moment, Russ thought the weight at his back was the entire crowd inside Ruby's pressing against him. But as soon as he smelled that musky, cinnamon scent, the same smell of pastry and fallen leaves, he knew he was wrong. That perfume only belonged to one person, and she was the only one pressing close. Russ closed his eyes as her hand slipped ito his pocket. As her fingers searched. And as her fist formed around the hair clip.

"Hello, you," he greeted, even before he saw her. He had opened his eyes, but they were trained on his glass on the bar.

It was going to be hard to look. Maybe he wasn't even allowed to look. What were the Christmas Eve rules in this place? What would happen to him if their eyes met? If he was nothing more than a mixture of Josie's memories and her imagination, would he dissolve?

He took a breath, deciding, all at once, that it would be worth it. That he could take breaking into a million tiny parts if he got one last look at her. It would, in fact, be the best way to go. Looking at Josie.

And so he raised his head.

But he did not disappear. Not in the first second or the next. Slowly, as time ticked, it became clear he was going nowhere. As that fear began to leave him, he could relax. He could really look. Really soak her in. That mouth curled into only one corner with a smile. The eyes, warm amber brown with flecks of ember yellow in them.

The differences were small. A few wispy gray streaks in that glorious chestnut hair. A tiny collection of shallow lines around her mouth. He hoped they were laugh lines. Wanted them to be. But somehow, he was also certain they were not.

"I've waited to talk to you for so long," she said, sliding onto the stool next to him.

The entirety of Ruby's Place faded, politely, giving them space. Almost as though the lights had been turned down everywhere, except for the small space between Russ and Josie, two seats at the bar. All of it—the bright green pine boughs and the red ribbon and the tablecloths and the candles, the piano, the dancing revelers—it all fell into shadow. Not Josie, though. She was as clear as anything Russ had ever seen. Everything about her was so real—the smell of her, the feel of her warmth as she sat beside him.

And judging by the way her eyes bounced across his face, taking him in, recording the moment, the same was true for her.

"Ruby tells me you've been coming every year," Russ told her.

Her eyes widened just a touch. "So you've seen her."

"Sure. She brought me a drink." He lowered his fingers like a crane onto the water glass and turned it back and forth slightly. He was so nervous. He wanted to grab both sides of her face and kiss her. And he knew why he could not.

"So you've talked about—this," she said, gesturing toward the darkness.

"What is…this? Your own imagination? A town-wide memory? Ruby was just talking about that. She…"

Josie took a breath, placed the hair clip on the bar, and reached for his hand.

For the first time in six years, her hands were touching his. And in that moment, *she* was his. The world was empty of everything but the two of them. The room around them didn't feel cloaked in shadow anymore. It felt gone. It felt like he and Josie were all that existed anywhere.

"I should tell you," she started, but her eyes filled and she stopped. Shrugged.

"It has been a glorious six years," Russ blurted.

"It couldn't have been," she said, all at once exasperated and disappointed. Her eyes begged him not to make her say it. The truth of what had happened that Christmas Eve all those years ago. *Surely you understand it all now,* her expression pleaded with him. "What are you *talking* about?" she asked.

"About Matthews. And the newsroom. And my apartment. Which is never without coffee. Not once, not in six years, have I had to grind beans. Always a fresh pot."

Her shoulders relaxed. "Right," she whispered.

"And that vacation. Tropical island, white sand, blue water."

"Just like we'd planned," Josie said. "We always talked about it. You and me, alone, warm nights…it killed me that we would never go."

"Not together. But you gave it to me, anyway. All on my own. When was it, two, three years ago?"

"Three."

"And the fact that I never got my feet wet when it rained. And the pillow was always cool under my cheek. And my car never ran out of gas. You did that, didn't you? You dreamed it—every moment—everything I lived. The perfectness of it all."

"Yes," she whispered.

"And never, not once in the last six years, did I ever feel alone."

A tear escaped at that point, and her upper lip turned a deep red.

"Because you were with me," he finished. "Maybe I didn't see you, but you were powering it all, making it happen. So in a way, you were there. Even if we weren't face to face."

"I wanted to be," she murmured.

"But we couldn't see each other," Russ said.

She nodded.

"Because I died," he finished, finally saying it out loud. "And you didn't want me to know it."

She wiped her cheek. "It's been so long. This year, when the holidays rolled around, I knew I needed you to realize what had really happened. What I'd done. And believe it. Your memory of me and mine of you were in conflict, sort of. Because I made you think the opposite had happened. That you had lived and I hadn't. You and I were both so fact-driven. We were taught to be. Every once in a while, somewhere, in the midst of my dreaming you onto a tropical island, I would get a stab in the gut, telling me I was wrong, doing all that storytelling outside of the facts. Leading you astray."

"It's why you came to Ruby's every year. You were hoping I would be here."

"I would think about meeting you here," she corrected. "And then I'd chicken out."

"What were you afraid of?"

"About five or so years ago, I realized what I'd done. I gave you this life, but you were grieving. Just as I was. I imagined you doing all the things we'd planned, I gave you what you loved, but without meaning to, I gave you my grief, too. I felt so bad about that." She said the last part to the hands now in her lap, not to Russ's face. "I knew," she added, still looking down, "I knew that this year, if I turned it into an assignment for you, I couldn't stand in its way. You would be here. No escaping it. No chickening out."

She finally raised her head, smiling warily. "You'd never give up on an assignment," she said.

"You've been lonely," he said, reading it in her face.

"What does that matter?" she asked.

"Of course it matters. It matters to me," Russ told her. "What, you think because you lived, you have no right to enjoy anything again? You're just giving me enjoyment?"

She tried to say something, but coughed as though the words were prickly in her throat.

"I saved you," Russ said.

"Yes."

"That's the best Christmas gift I've ever gotten. Knowing that."

She tossed her head back, putting her hand on her mouth.

"And this Christmas," Russ said, "we're going to give you a gift, too."

"You're not supposed to give yourself a gift on Christmas. Against the rules."

"Then I'm giving it to you," Russ said. "Me alone."

Her face twisted and she started shaking her head.

"Josie," he insisted, "I love you. Forever. I wouldn't change anything. Not one second of any of our time together."

"I'm so—"

"There's no sorry in this," Russ said. "None."

"But if I move on, what happens to you?" she whispered.

"Maybe it's time that I—" Russ wiggled his fingers, pantomiming a plume of smoke breaking apart and floating away. The same way the innkeeper had pantomimed her beloved Clarence breaking apart.

The mere idea of it turned Josie's eyes glassy yet again. Her nose deepened its shade of pink.

Ruby brought a cocktail glass and placed it between the two of them. Hooked a lime garnish on the edge.

"That's empty," Josie said. As though Ruby had forgotten to pour the drink.

"It's not," Russ said. "We're the ingredients. The two of us."

"Ingredients?" Josie chuckled through tears.

"That's what Hetty told me. Before I came in. That magic was made of ingredients. The two of us, we're—"

"—the perfect cocktail," Josie finished.

Russ nodded. "I would love to go back and live it all again," he said.

"You and me?"

"And the last six years. I wish I could go back and experience it again knowing you were behind it all. Could we do that? Is that allowed?"

She didn't answer immediately, only stared at him. Russ felt a twinge of fear creep in. He had expected her to smile with relief and agree. Was she really going to refuse?

"I have another dream," Josie admitted.

"I hope this doesn't involve me having to live in your pocket or something. There's usually a half-melted cough drop in there."

She laughed harder that time, running a hand through her hair. When it flopped back into her face, she picked up her clip and secured her hair at the back of her head.

"In this other dream I have," she started, "knowing what really happened doesn't make you disappear at all. Ever. Instead, you go back to the newsroom and you write exposés about Ruby's Place."

"What do you mean, exposés?"

"I mean, everyone on—my side—comes to Sullivan because they know this is a place where you can meet up with—" She gestured toward Russ.

He nodded, understanding.

"But there have to be so many people, in the—"

"—memory realm," he suggested.

"Right. The memory realm. Who don't know about this place."

"Who need a push," Russ said. "Like I did."

"What if your work could be directed at them? At the memories, I mean? What if you could draw *them* out here? And then no one would spend six years at a table missing someone?"

She smiled as she watched this sink in.

"I mean, human interest is a terrible thing. It's disgusting," she said, as clicking filled the air again. "But you wouldn't have to do it that way. You wouldn't have to be schmaltzy about it."

She glanced down, just as Carol the one-eyed pug trotted across the floor.

"Your memory won't let go of that old schmaltzy story of yours," Russ observed.

"That's not my memory drawing her in here," Josie said.

"Then who—" But Russ stopped when the pug made a beeline for the man who had been at The Page Turner earlier that day. The one who had leaned against the checkout counter as he'd talked to Rob.

"It was Scott's dog," Josie said. "The one I wrote the story about. The pug—"

"—Carol."

"Right," Josie agreed. "Carol. The dog. She disappeared from Scott's Aunt Joy's yard. She lived in a neighboring town and they were visiting her. Brought the dog to kind of run around the yard while they were there. Guess the pug was seeking greener pastures. Anyway, Carol somehow made it back in time for Christmas. The first story I ever covered. Right before the holidays."

The dog sat down beside Scott, begging for some attention. Scott simply sipped his hot cocoa, oblivious.

"There are all sorts of stories floating through here that haven't reached their end," Josie said, staring at Carol.

Russ felt sad, sitting there staring at the heartsick dog. But another man, one in sideburns and a polyester suit from the Watergate era, squatted, tapping his thigh. Carol opened her mouth into a doggy smile and trotted up to him, let him rub her ears.

"That's Scott's dad. Walter," Josie said.

"I met him earlier," Russ said, recalling their exchange just outside The Page Turner. "He said he was in charge of the…"

"…memory bank," he and Josie finished together.

Walter was a memory too. Same as Carol. Same as Russ.

"I suppose some would say you and me have gotten pretty schmaltzy," Josie said. Quieter, almost to herself, she added, "Or I have, at least."

"Maybe it's only schmaltz if you're looking at it from the outside," Russ supposed. "Maybe your own story could never be sappy or sentimental."

"Maybe," she agreed. Then, getting serious, "There must be all sorts of memories out there with stories that never got a final sentence. Maybe they need somebody to write the ending."

"Find the perfect last sentence," Russ added.

"No," Josie corrected, getting that look on her face like it had just come to her, the big revelation, her ah-ha moment. "They need somebody to write *up to* the last sentence. And then, with everything in place, the two people with the unfinished story, they could get together in Ruby's and write it themselves. Together. You know how people are. They kind of need to be led to where they need to be."

"Even me."

"Even you."

"You think I could write those stories," Russ said, mulling it over. "They would be distributed. In the, the…"

"…memory realm," Josie said.

"Right. And I would have one copy of every issue always sent here, to Walter."

"That's exactly where you should send them,"

98

Josie agreed. "On Christmas Eve, he opens up that memory bank."

"And then," Russ guessed, "if my stories were in there, in the memory bank, minus the last sentence, Walter could release them. And they could all sort of hit the Christmas Eve night air at the same time, calling everyone out. Current Sullivan residents and the much-loved memories both. And without understanding why, people here in Sullivan who had made no plans other than enjoying eggnog in fuzzy socks in their own living rooms would start dolling themselves up."

"Curling their hair," Josie chimed in. "Shaving their face. Digging their favorite tie out of the closet."

"And the memories—or the Christmas spirits, or however you're thinking of them—would suddenly realize they weren't a past-tense. Not entirely."

"I think you should put something in the last line of every one of those stories," Josie said, the embers in her eyes sparkling as her grin widened. "Something like, 'When you hear the whisper of these stories on Christmas Eve, know that…'"

"'…there will be mistletoe on Main Street,'" Russ finished. "'Just waiting for you to stand beneath. One last time.'"

"Yeah," Josie muttered. "That's my dream."

"And then?" Russ pressed.

"And then, even if I'm not actively thinking of you every single day, I'll know you're still going on. I'll know you're not…" She wiggled her fingers, mimicking the gesture Russ had made.

"It's a beautiful dream," Russ said. "Thank you for it. And for this, the best Christmas of all."

He took her hand and the lights returned. There they were, in Ruby's Place, as though it were still six years ago. The music and the laughter and the glasses clinking and the couples dancing. Russ led her out into the middle of the room, beneath a single bough of mistletoe. He could see every beautifully imperfect leaf, every white berry, every twist in the red ribbon holding it together. The music of one carol thundered to a close and the air filled with a slower, bluesier piano melody. Perfect for Josie. She wrapped one hand behind his back, put her mouth next to his ear, and she began to sing along, her alto voice serenading, "Please come home for Christmas…"

As they began to dance, as the soft white snowflakes fell all around Sullivan, as Hetty sipped her drink on the bench outside and Carol the pug got belly scratches from Walter, as Ruby mixed drinks and the past swirled all around the present, Russ's heart felt a kind of peace he had never known before.

A peace he knew that Josie had given to him. He tugged her still closer, knowing this would never happen again. Not for the two of them. But he knew that next year—and every year after—he would be here. A regular at Ruby's Place.

Eight
This Year, Christmas Eve

MATTHEWS WHISTLED "Silver Bells" as his footsteps and Russ's thunked down the carpeted main staircase of The Sullivan Inn. As he made his way, Russ wrapped his throat with a scarf. One of those itchy wool things, the sort his mother'd once insisted he wear every time he left the house, starting the very same moment she'd finished scraping the Thanksgiving dishes. That insistence would not let up until St. Patrick's Day.

Funny how the things you spent so much time fighting against always somehow wound up being the things you never could let go of. Even Josie had once teased him about it, his constant tugging at the scarves that were inevitably too tight, too rough. "What do they make these things out of, fiberglass?" he'd grumble, and she would laugh. "Why wear them at all if they bother you?" she'd ask, and he would look at her as though she'd forgotten who the President was. "What's winter without a throat rash?" he'd want to know.

And here, even now, he was still wearing them. Chuckling to himself about it, these days.

"You boys want to be here early tomorrow morning," the innkeeper called out. Betty, that was her name. Russ knew that now. Though he wasn't exactly sure when they'd exchanged names. So many jumps in time this past year, almost like he was playing hopscotch, skipping from one lovely moment to another, never a boring second in-between.

"And why, exactly, would we want to be here?" Matthews asked.

"Why for breakfast, of course," she said.

Russ recalled the orange cranberry waffles and the home-cured bacon, the thick strong coffee of the year before. "It's true," he said. "You don't want to miss it."

He expected a pleased smile to fill Betty's face as she waved them goodnight and disappeared through the door in the midst of the wall of keys. Instead, she slipped a winter coat on over her sweater, this one covered with appliquéd Christmas tree ornaments.

"I think I might see him this year," she said. "My Clarence."

She squeezed Russ's hand. It was one of those thank-you squeezes, the sort that was all at once too tight and also somehow clearly not enough, at least not on the squeezer's end. She smiled at Russ, and her eyes were filled with Christmas lights.

"I thought—because he'd never come to the inn—that something horrendous had happened," Betty admitted. "That we were somehow lost to each other. And I would never see him again. Not for all of eternity. But because of your stories…"

It came back to Russ all over again, that feeling he'd had the year before, that strange, anxious urge to protect the woman's feelings. "You shouldn't—well, *I* wouldn't expect miracles. I—"

But the innkeeper was already halfway out her own door. "That's exactly what this time of year is for! And besides, I know the work you put into this all year."

"But you said yourself you never saw any of my stories," Russ insisted. "Not one. And I have no idea if the morning editions were actually delivered to Walter, as we'd planned. Nothing is guaranteed. Not ever. Perhaps we need to work out the kinks this year. You can't assume…"

But he was talking to an empty parlor. Betty was gone.

Russ lunged through the door, the difference between the cozy warmth of the inn and the harsh chill of the December night making him feel like he'd been drop-kicked into an ice bucket.

Matthews stepped into place at Russ's side, smelling like Old Spice and newspaper ink. He grunted. "Woman can move," he commented.

"How can she already be nowhere in sight?" Russ asked. Mostly to himself, he added, "Why'd I have to tell her the plan before I left last year? The one about going back to the newsroom to write stories for the memory realm?"

Matthews guffawed. "Why would you not want to tell her?"

"Because she's so certain. And if it doesn't work…"

Matthews pushed Russ against his back, softly. "Come on," he said.

"I can't go in there. Ruby's. I can't. If it doesn't work, I'll…" Russ shook his head. "I'd rather not exist at all."

"What melodrama!" Matthews shouted, throwing his hands into the air. He had a strangely merry air about him lately. Ever since they'd gone on the road together, out here, to Sullivan.

"We trusted a *cardinal* to deliver the paper," Russ reminded Matthews. "Fly all the way to Sullivan. Really. A cardinal to bring each morning's paper to a ghost." Why hadn't he seen the holes in this plan before? Why had he been so sure it would work? What a fool he was.

Matthews gave him one of his best editorial grimaces and pushed him forward.

But not in the way of Ruby's.

They walked instead at a slightly different angle, not bothering to zip between cars. Matthews tugged Russ to a stop just outside the bank.

The sidewalk remained strangely empty. This was not a Christmas Eve sidewalk but an after-hours sidewalk, quiet enough that Russ could actually make out the faint buzzing of neon signs.

That was a funny thing, too, come to think of it. The way Main Street in Sullivan still had the old-fashioned neon signs.

Russ stuck his hands in his pockets and he gulped, the wool of his scarf feeling prickly against his throat.

And then, in the midst of the buzz, he could make out a clicking sound. Faint at first, but it grew increasingly louder.

He turned, and there she was. Yet again. Russ blinked snowflakes out of his eyelashes to make sure he had it right.

But yes, there she *still* was. Growing ever closer. Clearer, too, in the warm yellow streetlight glow: a one-eyed pug. Heading straight for the bank entrance.

"Carol, my girl, you enjoy this night even more than I do," Walter said, pulling a set of jingling keys from his overcoat. He paused to tip a hat at Russ and Matthews. One of those old-school hats with the brim and the feather on the band. The sort that had only, in Russ's life, belonged to grandfathers.

Walter jingled his keys into the door and held it open for his dog. A light popped on, illuminating the front tellers' booths, the line of offices off to the side.

Russ could see them both so clearly now with the lights on inside. He started to back away as Walter and Carol made their way toward the old original vault. The same, Russ knew, that held the town's memory bank.

Matthews popped a hand against his back. "Wait," he barked.

Walter had already disappeared. Surely he was inside the vault by now.

The night air grew colder around Russ. No cars lined the street. The storefronts were all dark. Final Christmas sales had already been made.

And no one, not one soul in the entirety of Sullivan, was still on Main Street.

At the end of the block, the red Ruby's Place sign popped to life. Russ only shook his head. Angela was doing as much wishful thinking as Betty, it seemed.

"How long do you propose we keep standing here?" Russ grumbled.

Matthews smiled, and it seemed to Russ that somehow the starlight was making a kind of white outline of his silhouette. "Until it happens," he said softly.

"Until what happens?" Russ asked. "I—" He stopped, tilted his head. "Do you hear that?" he asked.

"It sounds like a music box."

So faint. Those high-pitched, tinny little notes.

Before Russ could quite name the melody, one of the bank windows popped open in one almost violent burst.

Followed by birds. Not even a flock of birds. More than that. Hundreds, thousands of them, all of them showing out red against the streetlights. Cardinals, every single one that had ever built a nest in a Sullivan tree or bathed in a Sullivan rain puddle or offered a bright red spot of hope against a stark white winter freeze. They were all back, gliding beneath the deep velvet of the December sky.

Russ ducked his chin into his itchy scarf and raised his arms, afraid of being pecked to pieces.

As they flapped their wings, black specks flew off, dancing in the moonlight. Russ squinted through his fingers. Dirt? Dust? Hard to think straight, what with the chatter that exploded around him. Strange chatter. Incessant.

It wasn't the birds talking to each other, though. These were human words. A man's voice. Russ's voice.

How could that be, though? Russ strained, making out familiar phrases. That was his voice all right. He remembered these thoughts coming to him as he had typed there in his newsroom. In the streetlight, he could make out the pieces flying from the wings, some bigger than others. He could see the curves and the straight lines. All of it perfectly formed. Those black marks weren't made of dirt. They were type.

And the type did indeed form Russ's words. Every one he'd written all year. All those sleepless nights and pots of coffee. All those memories he'd strung together, to be published in the paper.

The cardinals disappeared into the night sky and the quiet returned.

"See?" Matthews said. "Your stories made it. They got delivered, correctly and on time. Walter just released them."

Russ glanced up and down the street, the air all around his head filling with the kind of white puffs that used to indicate he was panting in the winter.

Slowly, the magic of what he had accomplished flew off, following the path the last cardinal had taken as it had disappeared into the night sky. "What did it matter, though?" Russ asked Matthews, pointing at the empty street. "What did any of it matter?"

Matthews began to whistle again. "Silver Bells." He stopped mid-chorus. "Oh, sorry. You don't like carols, do you? Or decorations? Or schmaltz?"

Something about the mocking way Matthews said it popped a fire to life inside Russ. "I might," he snapped. "I might like it all if it amounted to something. If all the work did something. Helped someone. If Josie's dream was real. If it doesn't work, that would mean…"

Matthews cocked an eyebrow. "That would mean

that Josie really did move on. Completely."

"I always knew I'd never see her again," Russ corrected, the ice of the night invading every last particle of whatever was left of him. "I knew that. I knew we were going our separate ways. I knew that she was going to move forward in her life. I wanted that. I still do. But if this doesn't work, it means she didn't just move on. It means everything about us disappeared from her heart. It means that she *forgot*. That's what it means."

Matthews only stared at Russ.

In the distance, faintly, Russ could hear an engine.

The engine grew closer.

A car, some nondescript family variety, passed the two men. It came to a stop in a parking space just outside of Ruby's. The taillights darkened.

Another sidewalk click filled Russ's ears. He turned to see a woman in heels racing, moving so quickly her light blond hair, slightly curled, bounced against her shoulders.

A second engine roared by. A third approached, from the opposite direction.

And voices, scattered drops of chatter echoing against the cold night air. Laughter, too. Growing louder, growing closer. The trickle becoming a steady stream.

Arms in the air, waving to one another.

Two became five became ten. Twenty. Cars began to fight for space. With all the slots taken on Main

Street, they began to turn into the bank parking lot.

The lights inside the bank went out. The door swung open and Carol emerged, her hind end wiggling back and forth excitedly. Walter bent down to scratch her behind the ear.

In that moment, another crowd descended on Main Street. An entirely different rush. A quieter one, because cars weren't needed. In fact, they didn't seem to have arrived as much as they were simply brought into focus. "The memories," Russ said, astounded. "They came." They added an instant warmth to the entire street. But then, nostalgia was always warm, wasn't it?

Walter chuckled as he straightened up. "Come on, old girl," he told Carol. "This might very well be the night Scott sees you after all."

Matthews and Russ were walking again, both with that kind of anxious gait that said they couldn't quite figure out how to move fast enough.

Russ could have taken to the sky like a bird himself, he felt so light. What a thing to know for sure that he had always been this important to his Josie.

He and Matthews managed to stop at the entrance of Ruby's just before being swept inside. There beside them, by the door, was the same red wooden bench where Russ had met that old woman Hetty the year before.

"Hello, there, boys," she said, in a way that indicated she had acquired so much age that to her, *everyone* was now a child.

"This is my husband. Gent," Hetty said, pointing at the man beside her. A small man. Elegant. In a well-tailored suit and a knowing grin.

Suddenly, Hetty and her husband had extra cocktails in their hands and they were holding them out to Matthews and Russ. A thick layer of snow had fallen on their shoulders and hats, settled into the folds and wrinkles in their coats. Russ caught himself thinking they looked like a couple of snowpeople.

"No, no, not him," Hetty scolded her husband. "Only one is going to stay out here with us, remember?"

"Oh, that's—no, I'm not going in, either," Russ said, not sure why his words gave Hetty and her husband such confused expressions. "I had my face-to-face," he continued. "Last year. It's over now. Josie's gone. I'm going to be the regular now, instead of her." The very first time he had made the declaration out loud.

"No. I mean *him*," Hetty said, pointing at Matthews.

"Matthews can't be going in," Russ said. "Why would he? If Josie made him up, how can there be someone inside who misses him?"

He turned a bewildered face toward Matthews, who was offering such a strong closed-mouth grin, it puffed his cheeks out. They'd turned a bright red in the cold, too, giving him a jolly St. Nick look.

The realization settled like snowflakes on Russ.

"Josie's giving you someone. Isn't she?"

Matthews shrugged. "I simply suggested that it might be nice…"

"Actually, you can't, can you? Suggest anything, I mean. Not on your own. If you're a figment of Josie's imagination. Part of the story she dreamed up for me. So the truth is, Josie is the one that assumed anyone would like to be remembered. Loved that much. So she's dreamed up a loved one for you. Hasn't she?"

"She's something," Matthews said, "that Josie of yours."

And he disappeared behind the bright green door.

Russ stood laughing. Until finally, Hetty said, "Oh, can it, newspaperman. Aren't you ever going to sit?"

He accepted the cocktail glass. Squinted at her husband. "I thought I heard a music box a moment ago. You're an ingredient, too, aren't you? Aren't both of you? In the magic of this place?"

Hetty's expression was something of a mystery to Russ, one that he could not decode. But he also knew that inside that mystery was a story just waiting to be told.

"It really is quite a tale I have, *newspaperman*," Hetty said, as though reading his mind. Russ raised his glass a bit as he sat down, finding a place between Hetty and Gent.

Still, the crowds swarmed inside, the past and the present both. Still, the smell of toasted marshmallows bled out into the night air. Still, the sounds of carols thundered as they were sung around the piano. Still, Ruby rattled her cocktail shaker. Still, the stars twinkled, their clusters looking to Russ like boughs of mistletoe.

Russ reached into his coat pocket. There was no hair clip inside. Josie was somewhere else that night. As she should have been. But he did have a small notebook. He pulled it out and clicked his pen.

The cold of the night didn't bother him. And, strangely, neither did his scarf. "Go on," he told the couple on the bench with him. "I want to hear the whole thing. Don't leave out a single detail. I have all night."

RETURN TO RUBY'S PLACE

Want to know what Hetty told Russ?

Find out in *A Troublesome Heart*

Want to know more about Walter Drummond, the keeper of the town's memory bank?

Read *Tinsel Town*

Would you like to know how Ruby Westbrook returned to Sullivan and opened her own supper club?

It's all in *Ruby's Story*

Or would you like to start at the very beginning of the story and read straight through to the end?

THE ORIGINAL RUBY'S PLACE CHRISTMAS COLLECTION

The original four-book Ruby's Place Christmas Collection begins when Angela finds herself stumbling onto the past, and deciding that the very best Christmas present would be one more moment spent with a long-lost loved one. She soon learns that at Ruby's Place, the "spirits" are not confined to the dusty liquors behind the bar, and that the Christmas wish to see a special someone one more time is never made in vain.

Christmas at Ruby's

116

I Remember You

Sentimental Journey

The Gift That Is Ruby's Place

But so much story was left once that original series wrapped...

So the Ruby's Regulars series began. *Ruby's Story* tells the tale of how Ruby came to open her supper club. Each subsequent book focuses on a new regular: Elizabeth in *Rare Gems* and Walter in *Tinsel Town*. In *A Troublesome Heart,* the focus is on the very first regulars, those who occupied the building even before Ruby returned to town.

THE RUBY'S REGULARS SPINOFF SERIES

Ruby's Story

Rare Gems

Tinsel Town

A Troublesome Heart

Mistetoe on Main Street

Check **HollySchindler.com** for additional info and release dates of future titles.

Holly Schindler

Holly Schindler is an author, illustrator, and writing teacher…a storyteller through any means possible.

Her books have received starred reviews in PW and Booklist and have won both the silver medal in Foreword INDIES Book of the Year and the IPPY Awards. She is currently drinking too much coffee and singing carols far too loudly as she writes her next Ruby's Place installment.

Check out her socials, see the full list of published books, shop her courses and resources for writers, or subscribe to her newsletter(s) at:

HollySchindler.com